TRIPLE
DESTINY

Praise for *Triple Destiny*:

"A romantic journey that jets between the lush environs of Florida's Gulf Coast, the exotic locales of Bali, and the wide-open spaces of Australia. . . 'Triple Destiny's' fated lovers search for themselves and each other, aided by the specter of a child, in this uplifting story of love, birth and reincarnation."

Catherine O'Sullivan Shorr
Award winning Writer-Director,
'Warhol's Factory People'

"Triple Destiny is a heartwarming and engaging story about loss and rebuilding.

An unforgettable read!"

Catherine Greenman,
author of Hooked
(Delacorte Press, 2011)

I'm just a sour old cynic . . . but I love this book!

It's a travelogue of emotion in the magnificent landscape and spiritual culture of Bali, wherein wounded lovers heal and find each other, guided by the spirit of a much loved child. This highly romantic novel is so well written and so well grounded it has melted the ink in my sour old cynic heart.

Pat Kaufman: artist, author, and playwright.

TRIPLE DESTINY

Diana Colson

abbott press®

A DIVISION OF WRITER'S DIGEST

Abbott Press books may be ordered through booksellers or by contacting:

Abbott Press
1663 Liberty Drive
Bloomington, IN 47403
www.abbottpress.com
Phone: 1-866-697-5310

Because of the dynamic nature of the Internet, any web addresses or links contained in this book may have changed since publication and may no longer be valid. The views expressed in this work are solely those of the author and do not necessarily reflect the views of the publisher, and the publisher hereby disclaims any responsibility for them.

Any people depicted in stock imagery provided by Thinkstock are models, and such images are being used for illustrative purposes only.

Certain stock imagery © Thinkstock.

ISBN: 978-1-4582-0902-3 (sc)
ISBN: 978-1-4582-0904-7 (hc)
ISBN: 978-1-4582-0903-0 (e)

Library of Congress Control Number: 2013907862

Printed in the United States of America.

Abbott Press rev. date: 6/7/2013

To my mentors,
Mary Pengalos Manilla and Catherine O'Sullivan Shorr,
who helped me forge this vision into a book.

To my lifelong friend,
Dawn Aldredge Cohan,
who collaborated with me on a screenplay version of this story.

And to
my amazing family

Frank
Kevin
Sean
Marina
and
Lola Camilla

Contents

CHAPTER 1

Lancaster

THE BAD DREAM HAD SCARED her, so Katie Scanlon decided to get it right out of her head.

After she shoved her toys off to one side, she spread out a long roll of shelf paper. She grabbed a box of crayons and Magic Markers and plunked herself down on the paper. Scowling, she began to draw her nightmare in big wide strokes.

First, she drew her father driving some old kind of car. It was dinged and rusty and had no top.

Next, she drew herself there on the seat beside him. They were going down a country road. The car was moving so fast that the wind made her hair fly straight back.

In her nightmare, she screamed, *Daddy, stop! We're going to crash!* She scribbled her mouth wide open, but not one bit of voice came out.

Her father stomped on the gas and looked angry and mean. He headed straight for a cliff. The car's red fenders snapped out into wings. The thing whirled around like it was caught in a tornado. Then it shot straight up toward a big orange sun.

Terrified, Katie fell out.

Her heart started pounding. *I'm only six,* she thought. *If I fall to the ground, I'll die!*

Things looked pretty bad, but she knew what to do. She grabbed her bright yellow marker and drew in her pet canary. He streaked off to save her. His wings moved so fast that they blurred.

The bird grabbed her shirt in his beak. He pulled really hard, but he dropped her. She fell and fell for a million miles and then landed on the branch of a big green tree.

Gasping, she sat staring up at her dad. He was spinning around in his old red car, and he kept growing smaller and smaller.

If he touches the sun, he will melt, Katie thought, and she frowned.

"Put away your art stuff, Pickle. It's time for us to go." Startled by her mother's voice, Katie jumped to her feet, and the nightmare dissolved.

She rolled up her scary drawing and hid it under her bed. It was not for Daddy to see! She turned toward the cage and blew a kiss to her canary. "Bye, Mr. Sunshine."

Tweet, said the bird. His beady black eyes followed her as she skipped through the door and was gone.

Today was Katie's idea of an absolutely perfect day. She and her mother would be off by themselves, and her dad would be nowhere in sight.

Mother and daughter were headed for the Lancaster Library to see a film presentation on Bali. The two of them sat transfixed in the auditorium, watching a troupe of Balinese dancers move fluidly across the screen. Some of the dancers were barely older than Katie. They were gorgeous little girls tightly wrapped in brilliantly colored costumes made of brocaded silk, their graceful hands arched dramatically backward, and the toes of their bare feet curled upward like Aladdin's shoes.

"Oh, Mommy, they are so pretty!" cried Katie, and her mother smiled. Katie liked it when her mother smiled. It seemed like it had been forever since that had happened.

A flashy movement drew Katie's eye back to the screen. "What's that?" Katie jumped out of her seat to point at the screen. Her mother gently tugged her back into the chair as a fierce, lion-headed creature stumbled out onto the stage.

"It's the Barong," whispered her mother. "A mythical Balinese character."

"A what?" asked Katie. Her mother's response was drowned out, for the roomful of children was roaring with laughter.

Katie stared at the beast. It was a pretty weird thing all right. Its body was black, and its face a rainbow of gold and reds and oranges. Its back end seemed to move differently from the front. Katie spotted one pair of legs in the front and another in the back, so she figured two people had to be in there.

Mr. Front Legs wore an awesome mask with eyes that stuck out, long, sharp teeth, and a big red tongue. His hair looked like the scratchy tumbleweeds she had once chased on a road trip to Arizona.

Mr. Back Legs waggled a long, glittery tail. He kept kicking out to the back like a donkey. Mr. Front Legs kept whirling around, trying to see what Mr. Back Legs was doing. Katie clapped in delight.

After performing a couple of fancy steps, Mr. Back Legs comically plunked himself down on the floor, bringing the dance to a complete halt. Maybe that was what her dad meant by lead in the butt. Her dad said that to her when she didn't move fast enough. At the thought of her dad, a frown crossed Katie's face. Soon, she forgot, however, and joined the others in shrieks of laughter.

When the presentation was over and the lights came up, Catherine Scanlon took Katie to the shelves to find a book. "I want to dance like those pretty girls, Mommy. I want to wear those sparkly dresses. May we go there someday, Mommy?"

"This is an amazing world. Anything's possible. Just keep on dreaming." Catherine stroked Katie's sun-streaked hair, filled with love for her precious child.

After careful discussion, they chose one book and checked it out. It was the one that Katie liked best, for it had photographs of little Balinese girls in training to be dancers. Outside the library, as they descended the stairs, Katie clutched the book to her chest and hugged it tightly. "I can hardly wait to read my book. I love the way those dancers looked. They were *beautiful*!"

"They're just your age, Katie. In Bali, girls learn to dance when they're very young."

"Like I did?"

"Just like you, Pickle." Catherine smiled. Her passion was ballet. She earned her living teaching clusters of bubbly little girls, showing them how to point their toes, turn out their knees, stand tall, and be graceful. Her treasured Katie had been one of her most ardent students since she was three. "I love dancing," her daughter would say. "I love dancing more than anything else in the world."

Together, mother and child walked hand in hand down the tree-lined street, the setting sun warm on their backs. Catherine was glad it was summer. She loved the sultry, fragrant air and the sight of hawks circling lazily overhead. She loved the chattering of squirrels and the laughter of children out of school. She even liked their simple house—a wooden bungalow built in the 1930s, its white paint starting to peel. The little house reminded her of her grandmother's place, and that was comforting at times.

As they turned the corner, they saw that no car was parked in the drive. Katie giggled and did a little jig. "Good. Daddy's gone."

Catherine frowned. Since the plant had shut down last winter, Luke spent afternoons playing pool at the bar, coming home surly and mean, and yelling at Katie for the smallest infraction of his unpredictable "rules." He was becoming famed for his alcoholic rages.

"Daddy's not home. You can read to me," announced Katie. She clambered up the stairs to the front porch, her shoes making little clip-clop sounds against the wood.

"Eat supper first ... and get ready for bed. Then we'll learn about the beautiful dancers of Bali."

Katie wrinkled up her nose. "Oh, do I have to? Can't we read first?"

Catherine shook her head. "Nope. Reading time will be here soon enough. Go get ready."

Catherine unlocked the door, and the fragrance of chicken stew wafted over them. She scrubbed her hands at the sink and then dished out the stew from the Crock-Pot, while Katie washed up and scrambled into her pink pajamas. Catherine laughed. "Nothing like a book to make you hurry."

"I love books, 'specially when you read them, Mommy." Katie climbed into her chair. "May I say grace?" she asked, hoping that would hurry things along.

"As soon as I'm seated," Catherine smiled. After she took out a small breadboard, she sliced a baguette and carried it to the table along with a dish of yellow butter. After she placed two steaming bowls of stew on the table, Catherine pulled out her chair and said, "All right. Ready, set, begin!"

Katie kept one eye closed and the other one on her mother. "Dear God, thank you for the food we are about to receive. And thank you for showing me the pretty dancers. Amen."

Katie first buttered her bread and then tasted her stew, chattering all the while. "Don't talk with your mouth full," admonished her mother.

When dinner was finished, Catherine carried plates to the sink to be scraped and washed after reading time was over. Katie set about doing her pet-keeping chores, which involved the care and feeding of Mr. Sunshine, her small canary.

Now Mr. Sunshine was no ordinary yellow bird. He had been given to Katie by Mr. Wu, who ran the Chinese laundry at the end of the street. Mr. Sunshine was a genuine Chinese fortune bird, one that had been trained to select rolled-up paper fortunes from a tiny wicker basket. If you gave a coin to Mr. Wu, he would put a pinch of birdseed on his palm and show it to Mr. Sunshine. The little bird would then hop over to the basket and select one of dozens of paper fortunes. After the bird grabbed it with his beak, he would carry it back to Mr. Wu and then drop the fortune into the man's palm before he devoured the birdseed.

It was pretty amazing, or so the children in Katie's ballet class thought. Of course, the words in the fortunes were written in Chinese, but that did not matter. Everyone simply made up their own translations. That way they were totally happy with the fortune they received.

When Mr. Wu moved back to China, Katie inherited the bird. She solemnly promised to take wonderful care of the Mr. Sunshine, and she did. She cleaned his cage every day and gave him fresh seed and water. The little canary became a treasured member of the family. When friends came over, Katie charged just one penny to show off her bird's amazing fortune-telling skills. As for those who had no penny, there was always a bowl of copper coins waiting by the cage.

Each evening, Kati played the fortune game with Mr. Sunshine. Busy as she was, tonight was no exception. She dropped a bit of seed into her palm and thrust it toward the tiny bird. Mr. Sunshine cocked his head to one side and stared at Katie with beady little eyes before he hopped away to pick the perfect fortune. He dug through the wicker basket, selected one, and bounced back, the rolled-up paper clutched tightly in his beak. Katie opened her hand to receive the fortune, and he politely picked up the seed. Katie smiled. She was convinced that this fortune would be a great one, and she tucked it in her pajama pocket to read later when she was in bed. She felt her tiny bird was always looking out for her. She and Mr. Sunshine were the very best of friends.

Catherine smiled and patted her hand on the old leather couch. "Come on, Katie. Let's get started." The little girl jumped up on the couch, and her mother opened the fabulous coffee-table tome filled with beautiful color portraits of Balinese dancers.

It was a book meant for grown-ups, not children. Catherine had to edit the text, which was much too academic for a six-year-old. But the photographs—oh, the photographs! They were pure magic: brilliant costumes in rich, vibrant colors, golden crowns and diadems, flowers, sarongs, sashes, phantasmagorical masks, and headdresses. It was the stuff of dreams. Threaded through the book were photographs of wondrous little girls, all six or eight or ten years old, dressed in dazzling silks, their expressive eyes lined with black and their lips painted crimson.

These were the Legong dancers. They were trained from infancy in the graceful art of temple dance, taught to curl their fingers and toes up toward the sky and to theatrically roll their eyes from side to side. Pictures of the Legong dancers proved especially fascinating for Katie, for the girls were about her age and divinely dressed.

Catherine's reverie was broken by the sound of a car pulling into the driveway.

"Daddy," Katie scowled.

The car door slammed, and they could hear Luke swearing. "Goddamn it! Caught my thumb. Fuckin' car." There was a loud thud as Luke kicked the car door closed. *Oh, God, he's drunk*, thought Catherine.

"Hop into bed, Pickle. Here, take the book." Katie knew the routine and rapidly followed her mother's instructions. Catherine quickly ushered her daughter into her bedroom and closed the door behind her.

After she took a deep breath, Catherine went to the front door and opened it. "Luke, are you okay?"

Luke lurched up the steps, obviously inebriated. "No, I am not! I broke my goddamn thumb. I told you to get that door fixed. I told you!"

"The door shuts just fine," Catherine said evenly. "It just sticks a little when you unlock it."

"It slammed on my thumb!"

"Here, put ice on it." Catherine opened the freezer to get out some ice.

"Hell, that won't help my thumb. Ice is for putting in drinks. Where's the vodka?"

"Wherever you put it."

Luke started rummaging through the pantry. "What did you do? Hide it?"

"Maybe you drank it."

He swiveled to face her. "What's that supposed to mean?" When he saw the Crock-Pot, he lifted the lid. "What kinda slop are you feeding my kid?" He took a deep inhale and slammed down the lid. "Ugh. Chicken slop. I don't know how she eats that crap." Luke's eyes ricocheted around the room. "Where is Katie anyway? I wanna see my kid."

Catherine found herself feeling increasingly nervous. "Luke, she's in bed."

Luke moved toward the bedroom door. "Yeah? Well, she's my kid, and you are really pissing me off! I say it's too damned early for her to go to bad. Other kids stay up till midnight."

Catherine stepped protectively between Luke and their daughter's door to block him from entering.

"Leave Katie alone, Luke. She's tired."

"That's 'cause you work her like a horse down at that damned dance studio. I'm gonna see my baby, and you're not gonna stop me!" Luke swept Catherine aside and pushed open the door. The room was dark. Katie curled up on the bed, feigning sleep, her eyes scrunched tightly shut.

"Katie. Hey, Katie. Papa's home," Luke leaned down to kiss her. He smelled sour like he was made of smoke and sweat and something bitter. Katie did not like it when he smelled like that. Bad things happened when he smelled like that. *Go away, Daddy*, she thought, and squeezed her eyes even tighter. "Cute little girl," he said, stroking her tangled hair. "You're my cute little girl." Suddenly, he gave one of the strands a jerk. She flinched. For one brief instant, her eyes flew open and then snapped back shut. Her father grinned. "Hey, Katie, you're a good little sleeper just like your old man."

Catherine pulled Luke by the arm and coaxed him back toward the door. "I think I saw some vodka in the garage. A bit left in a bottle."

"Huh. Garage. What's it doin' out there?" Distracted, Luke stumbled back into the living room as Catherine shut Katie's door firmly behind them.

With her parents gone, Katie came back to life. She rubbed her head where her father had pulled her hair. Then she took the Balinese book out from under the bed, turned on a small flashlight, and studied the brilliantly colored pictures. As she turned the pages, she did her best to ignore her parents fighting in the background. Luke's voice drifted in beneath the door. "Damned kitchen's a filthy mess. Every roach in Ohio's gonna come for the party."

"I was just going to clean it up, Luke. I wanted to put Katie to bed first."

"Wife's job to keep the kitchen clean."

"I do keep it clean."

"Yeah? Well, there's goddamned food all over the sink." Katie heard the sound of plates crashing and flinched. She flicked off her flashlight and pulled the pillow over her head.

Luke's voice turned into a growl. "Bitch! Look what you made me do. Now there's food all over the floor. What kind of shitty housekeeper are you?"

Katie's eyes squeezed tighter and tighter, and she pushed the pillow against her ears. In her mind, she dreamed of dancers, beautiful dancers, young girls wrapped in brilliantly colored clothes. In her dream, Mr. Sunshine darted in and out between the dancers, delivering fortunes while warbling exotic Chinese melodies built upon the five-tone scale.

CHAPTER 2

The Lure of a Navy
Blue Bentley

NICK KONTOS BOUNCED ALONG THE wooden docks in a golf cart filled with scuba gear. The Gulf of Mexico glistened off to his left, its blue-green waters rimmed by a stretch of powder-white sand. It was at times like these that Nick felt certain he'd made the right choice. How many other jobs paid you to dive in the world's most fabulous spots?

He approached Gulf Marine Lab and pulled the cart around back. Then he backed it expertly into a spot that was marked with his name. Reserved parking was one of the few perks that came with a PhD. All those extra years in graduate school had mainly earned him a mountain of debt from which he was just emerging. Still, he was only in his mid-thirties, and his work had kept his body lean and fit. If he squinted at his reflection in the water just right, he could pretend he still looked twenty-two. Well, maybe twenty-eight.

As Nick unloaded a scuba tank, he stared at a gorgeous new

Bentley convertible parked next to his spot. The Bentley had cream leather seats and was painted an elegant shade of navy. At the front of its parking space, a workman was hammering a sign into the grass: *Reserved for Dr. Alexandra Knight*. Nick sighed and shook his head. "Oh, boy."

Nick tossed the scuba tank onto his shoulder. He carried it down a palm-lined walk and placed it in the storage room so that someone would refill it the following morning.

When he found a nearby receptacle, he emptied his pockets of small bits of trash—a chewing gum wrapper, the top to a water bottle, and a small plastic fork. Nick was meticulous about not throwing things into the Gulf of Mexico. Far too many seagulls had choked on objects such as these. He reached the front door of Gulf Marine Lab just as a spectacular blonde sauntered out. She was the kind of woman men noticed when she went walking down the street.

Alexandra—or Lexi, as she was known—was a brainy marine biologist who had attended university with Nick. They almost collided.

"Whoa there—"

"If it isn't Lexi Knight. I heard you were coming aboard."

Pushing oversized sunglasses on top of her head, Lexi stepped back to give him a slow, admiring look. "Well, well, well … Nicky Kontos. So we meet again." He figured she'd planned it that way, of course, but wasn't about to tell *him* that.

Nick was used to her antics. They had briefly been lovers, if you could call it that. Rambunctious bed partners would be a far better description. In spite of those youthful indiscretions, Nick was determined to keep this year's encounter strictly platonic. Lexi could be a pain—a gorgeous, rich pain, but a pain nonetheless. Nick had to walk a fine line with her. Her dad was the lab's biggest donor.

"We were bound to meet again, Lexi. I'm a fixture around here." Nick gave her a peck on the cheek. "How was life on Mykonos?"

"Not bad, Nicky. The sea was blue. The buildings were white, the swimsuits microscopic, and the ouzo divine. Three years were enough." *More than enough, actually.*

Nick motioned back toward the Bentley. "Daddy buy you a new toy?"

Lexi shrugged. "Well, he's got to do something with all that money."

Nick went right for the jugular. "How about something more substantial like a new boat for the aquarium?"

Lexi simulated a pout. "Hey, be sweet to Daddy's little trust fund baby. She deserves the best. Besides, he always liked you better than Mark."

Nick rolled his eyes. Oh, yes. Mark. How could he forget that egotistical jerk? "Where is that charming husband of yours anyway?"

"I left him on Mykonos. He's out of the picture. We're divorced."

"Do I offer sympathy or congratulations?"

"Congratulations, darling. Copious, endless congratulations. Marriage to Mark was a huge and spectacular disaster!"

Nick laughed. "Told you it would end up that way. Well, welcome back to Gulf Marine, home of the workaholics. Now you can focus on saving the seas." *Just don't try to focus on me,* thought Nick. *It's your dad I'm after. You could sure muddy the waters.*

Lexi grinned. "It will be great to be a working girl again! Gives purpose and meaning to my frivolous, jet-set life—or so says Daddy."

"The return of the prodigal party girl."

"Listen," Lexi placed a manicured hand on Nick's shoulder and looked him square in the eyes. She spoke in a low, cool voice. "It was fun. It is over. I am back on track."

As she ran her forefinger down his arm, Nick felt sun-bleached hairs jump to attention. Her voice turned into an unmistakable purr. "You know, you look good, Nick. Very, very good."

Nick jerked back his arm and frowned. "Now, Lexi, don't start that again. I need to have no complications when I work with your dad. Gulf Marine needs another wing, and he's got the clout to do it." Nick grabbed her by the elbow and steered her back into the building. "Here, let me show you what we've been doing while you've been gone."

The banter began once again. "Oh, I love a man who's strong and masterful," she purred.

"Yeah, sure."

CHAPTER 3

Maverick's Sports Bar and Grill

IN LANCASTER, TWELVE HUNDRED MILES away, Luke was drinking at Maverick's Sports Bar and Grill by three o'clock every afternoon, spending his unemployment check, pissed as hell at Catherine for having made him fall into this mess.

"Damned women," he muttered. "Always thinkin' of themselves. Selfish bitches." He downed the rest of his beer, and the foam left a frothy line across his upper lip.

The frizzy-haired woman at the end of the bar overheard him and glared. She looked angry, like one of those placard-carrying rabble-rousers you see yelling on the nightly news.

Luke stared her right back and growled, "What the hell are you lookin' at, bitch?"

"Up yours," snarled the frizzy-haired woman. With that, they both turned away from each other and ordered another drink.

Beer in hand, Luke moved to a table and fell into his own dismal stream of thought. He had spent the morning looking for work with no luck at all. Job pickings were pretty slim these days, and none of the available offerings needed his particular set of skills.

His mind kept returning to an upsetting issue: *If Catherine had only sold her damned dance studio, they'd be livin' on Easy Street by now.* Hell, she'd operated it for two years before they'd met, and it still only barely broke even. She should have dumped that place when they got married and given him the money to start his own shop. That's what a good wife would have done.

Or, hell—if her damned studio earned what she *said* it was going to earn, she could have kept it and just handed him the profits. But things didn't work out like that. The economy slowed, and dance lessons for kids kind of flew out the window. Oh, sure—Catherine made Dream Dancers, her studio, look like a happening place by renting out part of it to some weird-looking martial arts guy, a Japanese creep by the name Hiroki. Luke scowled. *I don't like that guy, and I sure as hell don't trust him. He thinks he's so hot, struttin' 'round in that stupid kimono.* Unexpectedly, Luke gave voice to his thoughts. "Well, kiss my ass, Hiroki, Kiss my ass!" he roared.

Maverick's collection of afternoon barflies awoke from their stupors to stare. The bartender frowned. "You got a problem?"

"Indeed he does," cried the frizzy-haired woman. "That man is totally crazy."

Luke chose to ignore them, cooling his anger with the dregs of his beer while his thoughts just kept on trucking. *It's all Catherine's fault. She takes in way too many students on scholarship. There ain't no free rides. No kid would get past me without payin'.*

What a mess. There he was, thirty-six years of age, with his classic car dreams in shambles. *Hell, if I was gonna get stuck in a regular job for the rest of my life, I could at least end up being foreman … or manager … or someone kick-ass important. Instead, I'm broke and out of a job. Sure never saw that comin'.*

Luke flagged down the bartender. "I'll take another. Make it a boilermaker."

With his drink sloshing over, Luke continued tripping down memory lane. *What the hell happened to my dream? Where did it all go wrong?*

He had started to work at the Kellycar plant when Catherine was pregnant with Katie. Seven years, and it felt like a hundred. His job was assembling golf carts. It wasn't the most exciting job in the world, but it paid okay. The plant also produced a line of small electric cars that were street-legal and boasted of zero emissions.

I don't give a damn about the environment, thought Luke. *I like muscle cars with big engines and glossy paint jobs, cars that turn heads on the streets.*

Before Kellycar, he had worked at a long list of body shops where he hammered out bumpers and fenders and doors. His dream was always to have his own shop, refurbish classic cars, and bring them back to their original razzle-dazzle. *Man, I've fixed some great wheels in my day—a Mercedes 190 SL, a '72 Eldorado. Hell, I even helped out on a '52 Rolls-Royce Phantom. Damn, that was classy!*

Pete was *the man*. He was the owner of Encore Classics. He was a master of restoration, and he was in charge of that Rolls. That was how Luke had met Catherine, when he was working for Pete.

It was maybe eight years ago. He'd been driving around in Pete's '64 Mustang ragtop, checking to see if the engine was running right, when he spotted this gorgeous lady with butt-length hair running down the sidewalk. At first, he had thought she was a hooker because her clothes were … well, kind of tight, with a little floaty skirt you could see right through. He knew right away that she had to be one of the fast ones. He knew 'cause Aunt Cissy used to dress like that when she worked at a strip club called Polecats. Aunt Cissy was one helluva wild woman who painted her face and jacked up her boobs and ran a little business on the side. When his mom stuck a knife in his dad, Cissy was the reason. Seems Daddy-o had a liking for painted-up broads. Next thing you know, Daddy was dead, Momma was behind bars, and poor little Luke had been dumped in a foster home.

"Like father, like son," announced Luke to the world. He stared admiringly at Catherine as she walked down that street in her skin-tight leotard and transparent skirt. Yep, she was one of the fast ones all right. He'd sure like to put his name in her little black book!

With that, he whipped that candy red Mustang over to the curb, put on his "innocent" face, and asked Catherine for directions to a place he'd already been to a hundred million times. Any old excuse to make conversation.

As it turned out, the lady was actually wearing dance clothes, not hooker stuff. She was a ballet teacher, and that was the way they dressed—hot. She gave him directions and then ran off to her dance studio a few doors away, leaving Luke and the candy red pony parked at the side of the road. Her studio was a place called Dream Dancers, and lots of little kids were waiting for her inside.

After that, he made it a point to come by on a regular basis, driving a different flashy car whenever possible. Pretty soon, the kids were waving at him when he drove up, and Catherine was going out with him for coffee. Luke prided himself on being a fairly smart guy, so he pulled back on the booze and pretty much behaved himself, except for smoking a joint now and then. He got his hair cut, picked up a couple of new shirts at T.J.Maxx, poured on the Old Spice, and took her out to Chili's in Pete's blue '64 Corvette.

"Hey, dude, you've gettin' to be quite the ladies' man," Pete teased with a grin.

Hell, it had worked. Pretty soon, he and Catherine had become an item. They got married on the beach, and before you know it, she was pregnant, which was definitely not part of his original plan. With a kid on the way, he was forced to get a "real job" at Kellycar, which he hated. Next thing you know, he went back to his true love, Marie Brizard, and her potent bottles of liquid painkiller, of which tequila was his favorite. And sometimes he'd do some drugs—a little nose candy now and then or maybe some ice or some bennies. Nothin' out of control. Luke knew he was way too smart to fall into a trap like that.

Damn it, he thought. *I did what I could to save up for my shop.*

Banked a hundred bucks every Friday. Catherine seemed okay with that. She never guessed that by Tuesday I'd pull it back out to buy beer and whatever, maybe a dime bag or two. Hey, a man's got a right!

Luke drained the last of his drink. *Shit, I did* more *than my best. Catherine didn't help me one damned little bit. If only she'd dumped her fuckin' studio! If only she'd put her husband first!*

He waved his empty glass at the bartender. "Hit me again, buddy. This time, make it a Jack."

CHAPTER 4

Think about It, Mrs. Scanlon. Think about It Very Hard.

A NGELICA LOOKED UP FROM HER computer to see a slim, lovely woman with long hair entering the waiting room of the office of Phillip Kleinberg—Marital and Family Law. *That has to be Catherine Scanlon, Mr. Kleinberg's three-o'clock appointment*, thought Angelica, and she crossed the woman's name off the list.

The secretary stood to greet the new client. "Mr. Kleinberg should be back any moment. He had to attend a client's funeral. May I bring you some coffee?"

"No, thank you," said the woman, and she took a seat.

Angelica settled her ample frame into the chair and returned to work. Periodically, she glanced over at Mr. Kleinberg's newest client in an effort to size her up. *She must be about thirty*, thought Angelica. She based that assumption on the woman's unlined skin and enviable dark hair, which cascaded to her waist.

Mrs. Scanlon kept placing her hand on her face, a gesture that only served to draw attention to bruises that were only partially obscured by dabs of concealer. To Angelica's prying eyes, these marks were clues to a dark and sinister secret. A juicy saga was about to unfold. Car wreck? Bicycle accident? Face-lift gone wrong? Jealous boyfriend? She'd know soon enough, for Mr. Kleinberg always had her type up his notes.

Angelica would never speak details to her friends, of course. No names. She believed with all her heart in client confidentiality. Still, sometimes, if a case was especially sensational, she would slowly reveal bits and pieces of the story in a discreetly edited version. Hers was a kind of fan dance in which words were brandished instead of ostrich feathers.

Angelica knew how to keep listeners on the edge of their barstools all right. Since she had become a privileged observer of marital skullduggery, she had been a star in Columbia's Friday night happy hour. Other chubby shop girls gathered around to hear her latest story. It was certainly better than replaying the soaps.

"Wow, that would make a great movie!" one girl would exclaim after an especially salacious revelation.

"Or an episode in a TV series!" another would chime in.

"Keep notes, Keep notes," everyone chirped in unison, happily avoiding their own plain lives.

It was Friday. The food was free, the pinot grigio was "two for one," and the weekly drama was unfolding courtesy of the offices of Philip Kleinberg—Marital and Family Law. Last week's episode had featured the tragically murdered Ashley. This week's episode might very well center upon the tale of beautiful Catherine Scanlon, using a fictional name, of course.

Angelica's thoughts were interrupted as Phillip Kleinberg swept through the door—tall, gaunt, and hunched over. He, too, noticed his client's pale bruises and frowned. "Mrs. Scanlon?"

The woman squirmed, clutching her purse like a shield. "Yes?"

"I'm Phillip Kleinberg. Forgive me for being late. Come in, please." He held the door open for her, guided her toward a chair, and then settled down behind his office desk. "What brings you here, Mrs. Scanlon?"

The client kept staring at the floor as if words might appear there in some sort of teleprompter. "I'm … I've come about Luke, my husband. He's … he's—"

Kleinberg urged her gently along. "Another woman?"

"Oh, no … nothing like that." His client shook her head, her voice muted. "Luke lost his job, and now he drinks. He drinks a lot. And when he does, he scares me."

"Does he use other drugs besides liquor?"

The woman looked startled. "Luke? Oh, no … I don't think so …"

Kleinberg fiddled with his pen on the bare-bones desk. He'd heard that before. Those were the men who were often the biggest users. "Go on."

The woman's soft voice belied the stark reality of her words. "Since Luke got laid off, he's become hostile and unpredictable. He's always checking on my whereabouts and makes terrible accusations that simply aren't true. He gets angry for no reason, shouts, rants, throws things on the floor."

Kleinberg shook his head, thinking, *Good Lord, please … not again.* He pulled a large yellow notepad out of his desk and began taking notes. "Is that how you got those bruises?" he inquired, his eyes glued to her face.

The client nodded. Tears started to fall, leaving little silver tracks across her injured cheek.

Kleinberg stared at the attractive young woman seated across from him and felt his anger rising. He remembered the words of his long-dead mentor, Professor Schmidt: "Stay calm. Don't get emotionally involved." In a domestic violence situation, however, that was one tough rule to follow, particularly when domestic violence escalated to death, which was exactly what had happened to Ashley.

"Are you looking for a divorce?" he inquired, hoping to God that she was.

Her answer was almost inaudible. "I want to feel safe."

Kleinberg frowned. "Are there children?"

"We have a daughter, Katie. She's six."

"I see." The sound of the lawyer's pen could be heard scratching across the yellow pad. Kleinberg paused to stare intently at his new client. "Do you think your husband might be dangerous to the child?"

"Katie? Oh, no—I don't think so. But she's leery of him, always walking on eggshells."

Kleinberg spoke in a cool, professional voice. "You do understand, Mrs. Scanlon, that your bruises are reason enough to call the police. I urge you to get a restraining order. If that does not stop your husband, then you must prepare to take more drastic legal action."

A look of horror flashed across Catherine's face. "Oh, no … I couldn't. The police? Oh, no."

The lawyer frowned. "What appears to be a safe situation could detonate in a flash."

"You don't understand. Luke would kill me if I called the police."

Kleinberg leaned back and stared at the ceiling. *Why were these battered wives always so damned resistant? This one reminded him of Ashley. If only he'd handled that differently, Ashley might still be alive.*

Kleinberg loosened his tie, took a deep breath, and leaned forward once again. "Mrs. Scanlon, be aware that your husband might kill you anyway." He rose up out of his chair, placed his hands on the desk, and looked straight into her eyes, his words coming in slow, measured phrases. "Let me be frank. I have dealt with situations like yours in the past, so I speak from experience. Your husband is an unemployed, angry drunk who has turned paranoid and violent. He has the potential of becoming as dangerous as a suicide bomber. I urge you to get out of this situation … now. *Get out!*"

The woman shrank back, bewildered.

Fired with conviction, Kleinberg became even more fierce and aggressive. He leaned even farther forward, and the heat of his words pierced her heart. "Mrs. Scanlon, take your child and *run!*"

"But—"

Kleinberg sank back in his chair, and his voice became cool. "Lord knows I'm not supposed to be saying such things. Forgive me. Unfortunately, one of my clients was murdered by just such a violent, unpredictable man. Her funeral was today."

"Murdered?"

Kleinberg nodded grimly. "It was a monstrous tragedy. That lady sensed danger but didn't do anything about it. I should have told her to run, to get away, but somehow, that didn't seem very professional. I behaved like a lawyer is supposed to behave, and for that, she has paid with her life."

"Oh …"

The attorney ran his fingers through his thinning hair. "Well, perhaps your situation is not so treacherous. Still, think about it. Make an emergency plan. You'll know if you need to use it."

The woman frowned. "Where would I go?"

"There are shelters. I could get you into one."

She shook her head. "I would be afraid to stay here in Lancaster."

The steel came back into the lawyer's voice. "Professionally, I am obliged to advise you of the legal route you should take. It's pretty straightforward. You need to notify the police, obtain a restraining order, and be prepared to move into a shelter. We could set all that up here in the office."

Kleinberg paused, drumming his pen on the notepad. He watched his distraught client. "Strictly off the record, Mrs. Scanlon, your situation could become lethal. Look, I'll deny that I ever said this, but my personal opinion is that you should take your daughter and disappear to some faraway place where the crazy son of a bitch can't find you. Think about it, Mrs. Scanlon. Think about it *very hard.*"

The woman looked stunned. "Oh, my goodness. Can't I just do what you said a minute ago? Can't I just get a restraining order?"

Kleinberg felt worn out and exhausted. "Frankly, I doubt it would do the job. The police can only enforce a restraining order if somebody violates it. That means you must be endangered at that precise moment for the police to step in. By then, it could be too late."

The woman wilted down in her seat.

Kleinberg frowned. "Look, I've overstepped my bounds. You know the man. Listen to your intuition. You'll do the right thing."

The woman moved toward the exit like a sleepwalker. Angelica nodded and chirped, "Good day, Mrs. Scanlon," but the client seemed not to hear. Phillip Kleinberg tossed his yellow notepad on Angelica's desk, where it landed with a slap. "Cancel my four-o'clock. My head is splitting," he muttered. "I'm headed for home."

Alone in the office, Angelica flipped through the pages of the yellow pad. As she studied the scribbled notes, her eyes grew wider and wider. Luke Scanlon? No kidding. He was the man who had worked on her brother's impeccable antique car. Could all that grinding on metal and pounding on fenders have made him a violent guy? Oh, the bones of a story were there all right. Change a name or two, embellish a little—

Angelica beamed. What a tale she'd have to tell at Columbia's Friday night happy hour.

CHAPTER 5

Balinese Dancers
Come to Lancaster

FOR DAYS AFTER SHE SAW Mr. Kleinberg, Catherine remained in a state of shock. In spite of the terrible things the lawyer had said, the situation at home seemed peaceful and not at all threatening. Catherine watched as her bruises faded slowly into oblivion. She waited for Luke to say something, but he appeared to have no memory of having hit her. Indeed, he'd even gone so far as to ask if she'd fallen off her bike. To this, Catherine had simply nodded, for she was in no mood to rock the boat.

As for the rest of it, Luke seemed okay, more or less. He even offered a small apology. "Hell, honey, that was just the liquor talking. You cook a lot better than all those other wives who just nuke frozen dinners."

Gee, thanks, thought Catherine.

Still, she had taken the lawyer's words to heart and had developed a plan. She squirreled a little money away and knew exactly how she was going to use it if Luke ever became violent again. As each quiet day passed, however, she began to think that her plan might never be needed.

Luke had apparently decided to cut back on the booze. Just beer. No hard stuff. Besides, there was talk about reopening the Kellycar plant, and he'd landed a gas station job for the interim. For Catherine, things were a lot better now that Luke had a job.

With Luke off at work every day, Catherine and Katie spent extra hours down at the ballet studio preparing for a magical event. Catherine had been instructing her classes on the dance dramas of Bali using posters and DVDs. To her delight, her young daughter had become completely entranced with the faraway land.

"Look at my book," Katie would say as she pointed out pictures to her friends. "These kids are dancing the Legong dance. They're pretending they're angels. And here—over here—the girls in the golden hats are doing the Bumblebee Dance."

Catherine was amazed at the impact it all had on her daughter. The child showed her treasured library book to anybody and everybody who crossed her path. "Someday I will dance just like that!" announced Katie. Catherine couldn't help but smile, for her daughter's enthusiasm was such that everyone believed her.

Today was the day, and the entire dance studio was bubbling with excitement. With Katie happily in tow, Catherine had arrived very early wearing her best studio clothes—a lime green leotard topped by a chiffon wraparound skirt, ballet flats, and no jewelry. She had pulled her long dark hair into a classic chignon and was feeling every bit like a ballerina. She finished teaching the 9:00 a.m. beginner's ballet class and went out to the street to look for the performers who were scheduled to arrive at any moment. Katie, of course, was glued to her side.

The Balinese family pulled up in their king-size van. The troupe consisted of mother and father, two sons, and two very young daughters.

Catherine greeted the family as Katie bounced up and down in excitement. "I'm so glad you could come perform at our dance studio. As you can see, our children are absolutely thrilled."

"It is our pleasure to be here," responded the father.

He opened the side door of the van, and the two boys carefully lifted out several traditional Gamelan instruments. These included carved wooden xylophones, metallophones, flutes, drums, and gongs. "Katie, show them the way to the auditorium," said Catherine. The girl skipped off, delighted.

Seeing the mother struggling under an armload of brilliantly colored silks and large folded umbrellas, Catherine ran to her aid. "Here, let me help!" Together, they carried these props to the stage where they would provide decoration.

On a second trip, the two women transported costumes into the dressing room while Katie and the two little sisters trailed behind carrying glittering headdresses. "Oh, Pickle, be careful!" gasped Catherine, afraid that she might drop the golden crowns and shatter them into a thousand pieces.

Catherine took the girls and their mother into the small dressing room lined with mirrors rimmed with lights. "Stay here, Katie," she said. "You can come get me if they need anything." Catherine went off to the auditorium, where she found the men of the family carefully placing their Gamelan instruments. *Perfect*, she thought. *All my students will all be able to see.*

Back in the dressing room, Katie solemnly studied the Balinese children as they got ready for their performance. She figured one of the girls was about her age, the other maybe a year or two older. Both had long, glossy hair the color of shiny black satin, tied at the back with a ribbon.

As the mother began painting her youngest daughter's face, Katie's eyes grew as big as saucers. *She's done something weird with her eyebrows. Pulled out all the little hairs, I think. Oh, my goodness, she's drawing the eyebrows back in, but way up higher.*

Working first on one daughter and then the other, the woman carefully traced black eyeliner all around their eyes and smudged their lips with bright crimson. Last of all, she brushed on a bit of rouge and a little smidge of powder. *Boy, do they look pretty,* thought Katie. She kept wishing the nice lady would give *her* a paint job like that, only maybe not the eyebrows.

Their faces stage-ready, the two little girls were now tightly wrapped in dazzling sarongs held firmly in place by wide golden sashes. Katie held her breath as headdresses were pinned into place and transparent scarves were attached to their shoulders. *Those must be their angel wings,* she thought. In no time at all, the children had magically changed into real Balinese dancers who looked just like the pictures in her book.

Catherine stuck her head in the dressing room door. "We've got the stage all set up. Better get out front, Katie. You don't want to miss anything."

"Showtime!" yelped Katie. She scampered off to join the others in her ballet class, utterly beside herself with excitement.

Peeking through the curtains, Catherine could see her young assistant, Larissa, shepherding the line of giggling six-year-olds into the auditorium. Dressed in pale pink leotards and tights, their cheeks flushed from exertion, these aspiring little ballerinas looked like a string of laughing cherubs. Katie had jumped to the head of the line, where she bounced up and down shrieking, "Miss Larissa, wait 'til you see the dancers. They're so beautiful! They're so beautiful!"

"Cool it, Katie," scolded Larissa.

The group whispered and wiggled and tickled their way into the auditorium as Larissa unsuccessfully tried to settle them down. The little ballerinas plunked themselves down on the floor as a small group of boys shuffled in, fiercely decked out in aikido uniforms. These energetic young lads poked at each other and jostled for position until Hiroki, their sensei, quieted them with one single shake of his head.

Larissa shook her head in amazement. "Good lord, how does he *do* that?"

Last to file in were a handful of parents with stroller-aged children. The adults seated themselves on folding chairs at the back, and the room hummed with happy anticipation.

The show was about to begin when Luke Scanlon entered, sullen and scowling. Hiroki stared at Luke, and a cloud washed over his face.

Chapter 6

In the Eye of the Beholder

THINGS HAD NOT GONE WELL for Luke that morning, and he was feeling shitty. He'd just been laid off minutes ago from that crappy gas station job for sneaking a joint, of all stupid things. He was hot and bothered and needed something to cool off, so he pulled up to a convenience store and grabbed a six-pack, half of which he downed while he was driving to Dream Dancers.

He hadn't planned on going to the studio. He'd planned on being at work. He was definitely in no mood for Catherine's Balinese dance crap. His only mission was to pick up Katie and get the hell out of there.

After he slipped into the building, Luke found a spot away from the others where he could lean against the wall. He was startled to see Catherine slip out from behind the wings to talk to that sneaky little Jap. *What was his name? Oh, yeah ... Hiroki.* His stomach turned as he watched the two of them whispering at the side of the room. There was something funny going on, and he sure didn't like that creep. The yellow-faced weirdo was always bringing Catherine some sleazy little gift—a single flower, a polished stone. Something freaky about a man who wears kimonos and gives fuckin' presents to some other guy's wife.

Why does Catherine go for all that stupid shit? There she is, whispering secrets in the little Jap's ear. Christ, she's leading the guy on right in front of a roomful of people. What the fuck's going on?

Catherine slipped back behind the curtain. Hiroki closed the auditorium doors and moved backstage to run the lights. In the darkening room, Luke found himself engulfed in waves of claustrophobia, trapped in a room with a bunch of sweaty little kids. That wasn't his plan. He wanted to catch fish, drink beer, and have his little girl all to himself. Go hiking maybe. Anything to get his mind off of losing that stupid job.

Unaware of Luke's unexpected arrival, Catherine stepped out to the microphone to introduce the performance. As she did so, the Balinese father and his two sons emerged from the wings to sit cross-legged behind their instruments.

Luke frowned as the eldest son strode to the microphone, a serious lad of fourteen with a resonant voice that belied his years. "Balinese dance was created as an offering to the deities," intoned the boy. "For the Balinese, dance is a medium for traveling between the world of form and the world of spirits."

"Bullshit," muttered Luke.

The auditorium lights went out, and the music abruptly started. The room was filled with a shimmering, rhythmic, hypnotic sound of the Gamelan.

As the front curtain opened, Katie held her breath. The stage had been fixed so it looked like a fairy tale. Golden umbrellas had been opened, and sheets of bright cloth were pinned over the black curtain. The two little dancers emerged barefoot from the wings, their eyes shifting dramatically from side to side, their headdresses sparkling.

Their bodies were wrapped so tightly they could hardly move, but move they did, taking the tiniest of steps. To Katie, the music sounded just like a trickling waterfall. The two little girls drifted magically across the stage, waving glittering fans and moving their arms like ribbons. Katie knew she would never forget it, for it was the most beautiful thing she had ever seen.

Luke, however, was having quite a different experience. To him, these very same Balinese dancers looked like painted hustlers working the street. Their skin-tight costumes were garish and cheap, and their provocative moves were sexually arousing. *I'm no stranger to the life,* he thought. *Aunt Cissy used to dress like that. Skirt pulled tight around her ass. Shakin' it around like an engraved invitation. She might just as well have shouted, "Stick it to me, baby. Stick it to me!" Daddy couldn't help but take the bait.*

Luke voiced his disgust to no one in particular: "Who the hell would dress a kid like that?" he snorted. A pregnant young mother seated nearby turned her head and frowned.

Stupid fornicating bitch, thought Luke.

Seated thirty feet away, Katie knew nothing of her father's dark thoughts or indeed of his arrival. She was lost in the land of enchantment. From things her mother had said, she knew the Legong was a dance about angels, one that was only danced by very young girls. Katie stared at the beautiful children and sighed. *Oh, I wish I could be an angel.* She loved the bright silk sarongs. She loved glittery headdresses that were made of red leather and gold. She loved the little red tassels that dangled over each dancer's ears. She thought the girls looked just like princesses from a faraway land.

Watching the very same performance, Luke snorted in complete disgust. *Cissy used to doll up like that. Big red lips, black around the eyes, ass stickin' way out behind. What kind of a come-on is that?*

"Those damned kids look like hookers!" he exploded.

The pregnant woman turned in her chair to look at him. "Hush," she said and frowned.

The performance went on as if nothing was wrong. Slender arms were in constant motion, while tiny fingers bent backward into impossible positions. Luke was blind to the dancer's beauty, for his mind was on an unstoppable roll. Like some weird heat-seeking missile, it dug into things that had happened long, long ago, things that made Luke eternally angry, things that had wrecked his life.

Momma was wrong, crazy wrong. Stabbed Daddy in the heart, she did. But he was just doin' what a man's gotta do—followin' his cojones.

Luke pulled a beer out of his back pocket and popped the lid. The music was driving him nuts. All that hammering sounded like nails in a coffin. He leaned against the back wall of the auditorium and chugalugged the can, and then he wiped his mouth with his hand. The smell of Budweiser floated out into the room, but the audience was too entranced to notice.

Luke was drowning in a tsunami of thoughts, all of them bitter, all of them black. *And what did Momma get for killin' my dad? A lifetime in jail, that's what. An' little Lukey-boy got sentenced to ten years in a foster home. All on account of a painted whore. All on account of dear darlin' Aunt Cissy.*

Gamelan music rained down as exotically costumed children floated gracefully across the stage. Katie sat spellbound, unaware of what was about to come.

Abruptly, Luke stepped away from the wall and growled: "That's it! I'm outta here!" Searching the crowd for his daughter, he sighted her near the aisle. "Katie! Pssst, Katie!"

"Daddy?"

"Quick! Get up!"

"But Daddy—"

"Come on. Let's go!"

Katie's lower lip quivered. "But Daddy, I'm watching!"

The sounds of the xylophones built to a crescendo, and Luke's whisper dissolved into an angry hiss. "Get up *now*, young lady!

Move it!" His words were lost to everyone but Katie, who was all too familiar with the sharpness of that voice.

Fighting tears, Katie got to her feet and stepped over and around other children seated near her. Her father reached for her hand, but she jerked it away, scowling.

A dark look came across Luke's face. He grabbed his daughter tightly by the arm and ushered her out the door. Through it all, the audience remained riveted by the captivating performance.

Only one person noticed Katie's reluctant departure. It was Larissa.

CHAPTER 7

Bye Bye Birdie

SEATED AMONG THE CHILDREN, LARISSA frowned. She got up and slipped into the wings to find Catherine. "Were you expecting your husband to pick up Katie?"

Catherine looked at her, startled. "No, I wasn't. Why do you ask?"

"Well, he was just here."

"Good lord!"

Catherine rushed from the auditorium and out onto the sidewalk. She could see Luke's car disappearing down the street, Katie's tear-stained face peering out the rear window. A wave of fear swept over her.

She ran to her bicycle, which was chained to a lamppost along with Katie's bike. She jerked at the chain, but it was locked. She raced back into the building and collided with Larissa backstage.

"Catherine, what can I do to help?" the girl whispered.

"I've got to get home. Where's my purse? The bike keys are in it."

"It's there under the chair." A distraught Catherine grabbed for her purse as Larissa continued, "Look, I'll drive you."

"No, no, one of us has got to stay. It's only a couple of blocks."

Larissa looked worried. "Are you sure? He seemed awfully angry. I'd be glad to help."

"No, please. I'm sure everything's fine. I should be back in just a few minutes."

Hiroki stepped away from the light board and said in a low voice, "Want me to come with you?"

Catherine shook her head. "If you showed up, it would just make things worse. Look, if I'm not right back, please thank the performers."

Hiroki frowned. "Are you sure?" he said, but Catherine was already gone.

After she fumbled with the bike lock, Catherine unhooked the chain and hurled it to the ground, which caused Katie's bike to crash to the pavement. Ignoring the fallen bike, Catherine grabbed her own and pedaled furiously down the street, her thoughts striking terror in her heart. *What if Mr. Kleinberg was right? What if Luke tries to hurt Katie? Oh, God!*

Luke dragged a miserable Katie up the steps of their small wooden house. Reaching the doorstep, he used his free hand to unlock the front door. Once inside, he rummaged through the closet, unearthed a bottle, and poured himself a jelly glass of amber liquid.

As she watched him, Katie grew so frightened that she could hardly breathe. Mr. Sunshine would know how to keep her safe. Sniffling, Katie went to the birdcage and removed her yellow canary. She felt his tiny heart racing, kissed him, and stroked his feathers. "Hi, Mr. Sunshine. Kissy-kissy, Mr. Sunshine—"

The canary responded with a trill and a poop. Katie stared at the spot on the floor. "Yuck!" she said. She looked nervously at her father, unsure of how he would take Mr. Sunshine's horrible breech of etiquette.

Luke did not even notice. After he gulped down his drink, he stormed into the bedroom and started yanking suitcases from the closet shelf. "Put that goddamned bird away!" he shouted over his shoulder.

Katie flinched. She hurriedly shoved Mr. Sunshine back in his cage and made a feeble effort to wipe the floor with a paper napkin but only succeeded in making more of a mess. Flustered, she accidently left the cage door slightly ajar.

Luke glared at his daughter through the open bedroom door. "And *you*, little girl, get out of that sleazy outfit *right now!*"

Katie looked down at her leotards. She was proud of her pale pink ballet suit. Had she gotten spots on it or something? Luke roared, "Damn it, Katie. Take those clothes *off!* You look like JonBenét Ramsey."

Katie was bewildered. "Who's that, Daddy? I don't—"

Luke's face became flushed and twisted. "She's a kid who was murdered because her mother dressed her up like a slut!"

Katie started to cry. "Daddy—"

"Get jeans. Get T-shirts. Get a sweater and a jacket. And get out of that damned pink thing!"

"It's a leotard, Daddy. You know it's a leotard."

"It's trash! Get out of it! We're going camping. It's time you got outdoors with your dad."

"I don't want to go camping, Daddy. I want to stay here."

"Well, guess what! You're going. Shut up!"

The front door burst open, and Catherine entered. Katie ran to her mother and buried her face in her skirt. Catherine stroked her daughter's head and looked around warily, taking in her husband's reddened face.

"Luke, what's going on?"

Luke was all defiance. "What do you care? Look at you, all decked out like a pole dancer!"

Catherine nudged the frightened Katie behind her. Speaking

softly, she tried to get control of the situation. "Luke, please. Don't start that again!"

Luke ran his hand through his hair. "There you are, parading down the street like a prostitute. What kind of mother *are* you?"

Catherine fought to stay calm. "These are athletic clothes. I teach dance, remember?"

Luke's voice dripped with sarcasm. "I'll bet you teach a whole lot more than dance! I'll bet you teach some real fancy moves to that weaselly little Jap!" Fists clenched, he took a step toward her.

Catherine stood her ground. "You're drunk."

In a flash, Luke crossed the line between angry and deranged. "Booze is not the problem. *You* are the problem, bitch! You and that weird martial arts guy. I saw you whispering secrets in his little yellow ear."

Katie whimpered, "Mommy—"

Catherine backed away, moving Katie to one side. "I don't know what you're talking about."

Luke continued to stalk his wife. He shoved her against the couch, his voice filled with molten rage. "You think you've pulled one over on me, don't you? But I know all about you and your slanty-eyed lover boy."

Luke twisted Catherine's arm behind her back and shoved his face close to hers. His eyes narrowed, and his voice squeezed into a predatory hiss. "Know somethin', Catherine? You're no different than my slutty Aunt Cissy. My daddy died because of her, and you're turnin' into her spittin' image. You've got the morals of an alley cat, and you're teachin' all that shit to our little girl."

"Oh, Daddy, she's not!" cried Katie.

Luke snapped, "Stay outta this, baby." He twisted Catherine's arm even harder, and she gasped in pain. Luke glared at her in disgust. "Maybe Momma was right. When your spouse starts cheatin', stick a knife in their heart!"

With that, Luke hauled off and gave Catherine a brutal slap, and she keeled over onto the couch.

Katie flailed at her father. "I hate you! I hate you! I don't want you for my daddy. Daddies are supposed to be nice!" Luke swatted the child aside. She crumpled to the floor, upending the birdcage. As it crashed to the ground, the cage door sprang open. There was a noisy flutter of wings, and Mr. Sunshine began nervously chirping.

Catherine watched as her husband's personality dramatically reversed. Luke's voice turned into a pathetic wail filled with self-pity and tinged with remorse. "Oh, God, Catherine. I love you so much. Why do you keep doing these terrible things to me? I've lost that stupid job, and I can't take your damned bitching. I can't take your dressing like a whore, and I sure as hell can't take your screwing another man. I love you. Oh, God, I love you! Look what you've done. Look what you've done." In drunken confusion, he lurched toward the street, leaving the front door wide open behind him.

Katie crawled over to her mother and whimpered, "Mommy, are you okay?"

Catherine grabbed her daughter, held her tightly, and rocked her back and forth. "Oh, honey, your daddy wasn't always like this."

Suddenly, there was a flash of yellow and the sound of fluttering wings. Katie gasped, "Mr. Sunshine!" The tiny bird flapped twice around the room and soared through the open door. Katie looked on in horror as Mr. Sunshine flew out of sight. In the distance, Luke's car could be seen careening up the road, its tires screeching.

Catherine drew the door shut and locked it. She sank down on the floor, pulling Katie beside her, and took Katie's tearful face in her hands. "Baby, listen. We've got to get out of here ... fast. Daddy could hurt us. It's not safe for us to stay. We've got to fly away like Mr. Sunshine."

Katie began to wail, "But we don't have any wings!"

"Well, we're going to sprout them. Pack up, baby. We're hitting the road." When she saw the open suitcase on the bed, Catherine dumped Luke's clothes out on the floor and began packing her own things.

"But Mommy, what about Mr. Sunshine? I love Mr. Sunshine. I want him back."

"There's not much we can do, Katie. Once they get out, birds are almost impossible to find."

"But he's my best friend!"

"I know. I know. But he's smart, and he'll be okay."

"Maybe he'll try to find us?"

"Bet he will ...or maybe one of his cousins." Catherine turned to hug Katie. She could feel the little girl shaking. "Okay, take a deep breath and get packing. Okay?"

Tears welled up in Katie's eyes. "I miss Mr. Sunshine."

"Of course you do, but he'll always live in your heart. Birds have a way of doing that, especially Chinese fortune birds." Catherine tilted her daughter's tearful face upward and gazed in her eyes. "Hey, you're my big, brave Pickle. How about a smile?" Katie did her best to oblige. "Now put the little stuff in your backpack and the big stuff in the rollaway."

Katie frowned. "Oh, look at your face, Mommy. It's turning all red."

Catherine ran to the bathroom mirror and touched her wounded cheek. "Better get me some ice."

Katie ran to the freezer and pulled out a handful of cubes. "Ice worked on my knee, Mommy."

"Then ice will work on my face." Catherine rubbed a cube on her cheek with one hand while she selected cosmetics with the other. "Keep packing, baby. We've got to get out before Daddy comes back."

Katie's lower lip quivered as she looked at her mother for reassurance. "Are we going to have a good time, Mommy?"

Catherine smiled, radiating utter confidence. "Of course we are, honey. We're going to have a *great* time. Pack up."

In her heart, however, Catherine was racked with uncertainty.

What if running away was the wrong thing to do?

Chapter 8

Zigzag on the Bus

IT WAS LATE IN THE afternoon when mother and daughter arrived by taxi at the Lancaster Bus Station, Catherine carrying her tan canvas tote over one arm, along with her red purse and jacket. She wrestled with the black rollaway bag, which was large and awkward. Katie followed in her mother's wake, struggling with a much smaller rollaway with wheels that kept getting stuck. Both mother and daughter wore blue jeans and orange T-shirts, to which Katie had added a turquoise windbreaker and flowered backpack.

"We need tickets, Mommy."

"Wait a minute. I've got to make a call first." Dragging their cases, Catherine and Katie headed for the last surviving pay phone in the bus station, all others having been vandalized. Catherine pulled out a credit card and dialed. Luke's voice was heard as the answering machine clicked on. *You've reached the Scanlons. Leave a message.*

Catherine paused. This was it. She had to say it right. She took a deep breath and began, "Luke, I don't feel safe anymore. Neither does Katie." Her voice started to shake, and she clapped her hand

45

over the mouthpiece. She took another deep breath, and her voice became steely. "Luke, we're leaving. Don't try to find us. It's over, Luke. It is over!"

Catherine slammed down the phone. Katie took her hand and found it was shaking. "What's over, Mommy?" the little girl frowned.

"Come on, sweetie. Let's go get our tickets."

An enormous man took forever at the ticket counter, but finally, he made his purchase. He waddled off toward the boarding area, and Catherine stepped up to the window. The ticket seller was rude and abrupt and obviously not enamored with his career.

"Where to, lady?"

"I'm not exactly sure," answered Catherine.

The man looked exasperated. "Are you pulling my leg?"

Catherine had decided to travel a nonsensical path. She figured that if there was no logic to their escape route, Luke could not possibly track them. Being unpredictable was her way of hiding.

"We just want to buy a short trip. Maybe fifty dollars' worth."

"And you don't even know where you want to go?" growled the ticket seller. "That's weird."

"Oh, no, it's not," piped up Katie. "My teacher said that when school starts, we've all got to tell where we went this summer."

Catherine couldn't help but smile at her daughter's ingenuity. She gave Katie the thumbs-up sign before she turned back to the cranky ticket seller. "Yup, it's part of a school project. My daughter is going to tell her second-grade class all about her travels on a bus."

"You sure got a ton of luggage for a short trip."

Mother and daughter nodded in unison. "Ah, that's called method acting," said Catherine. "We're pretending that we're off on a long, long trip."

The man shook his head. "And I thought I'd heard 'em all."

Catherine placed three bills on the counter. "So ... we want a fifty-dollar adventure. What have you got?"

"Want to go east or west?"

Catherine looked down at her daughter and asked, "Which way, Pickle?"

Katie shrugged. "Which way's the moon?"

"Hmmm. Moon over Miami. That's east. Well, southeast." Catherine turned back to the ticket seller. "We'll take something in the direction of Florida."

"Forty-six dollars gets you as far as Springfield, Ohio."

Catherine shrugged. "Okay."

The man shoved two tickets across the counter. "One child, one adult for bus thirty-eight. Loads in five minutes."

"Got it." Catherine picked up the tickets. She and Katie coaxed their unwieldy rollways across the passenger waiting area.

"What are we going to do in Springfield, Mommy?"

"We'll catch another bus. We're playing a new game. It's called Zigzag. That way Daddy can't find us."

Katie grinned. "Cool!"

With a squawk, the loudspeaker suddenly came to life: "Bus thirty-eight for Springfield, Ohio, is now loading."

As they moved toward the bus, a heavyset woman seated on the bench looked at them quizzically before she turned to her skin-and-bones husband. "Isn't that Luke Scanlon's wife?"

The man glanced up and saw Catherine and Katie boarding the bus. "Sure looks like her. Yup, that's their kid. She's sure gotten big. Reminds me—I've got to call Luke and tell him that Kellycar is scheduled to open back up in September."

"Bet he'll be glad to hear that."

"Bet he will."

The zigzag bus trip to Florida took three days, and it was tedious and tiring. Every few hours, Catherine and Katie would get off and change buses in hopes that their path would prove untraceable.

In Kentucky, they both fell asleep in the waiting room and missed their bus. Catherine awoke with a start and couldn't see Katie, who had curled up on the bench behind their suitcase.

Catherine gasped, "Oh, Katie, I've lost you!"

The little girl sat up and sleepily rubbed her eyes. "You haven't lost me, Mommy. I'm right here beside you."

"Oh, honey, you scared me," her mother said and sighed in relief. "Stay with me, Katie-girl."

The child nodded solemnly. "Oh, Mommy, I will. I promise."

They turned in their tickets for new ones. It didn't much matter *where* the next bus went as long as it was in a southern direction. They had no clear idea of their final destination, except that it would be somewhere in Florida.

It was a strange kind of plan, Catherine had to admit, but she felt it would work. If *they* didn't know where they were going, how could Luke possibly figure it out?

Katie passed the hours staring out the dirty window of the bus. Sometimes she thought she saw flashes of yellow wings. Could it possibly be that Mr. Sunshine was flying right alongside them? Hey, he was a pretty cool bird, and he loved her a lot. It *might* be Mr. Sunshine, or it might be some other bird wearing Mr. Sunshine's feathered suit. Whatever the case, Katie felt her Chinese fortune bird was right there beside her, delivering the perfect paper fortune for their zigzag trip.

For Catherine, the monotonous sound of bus tires hitting the highway seemed to say, *"Get-away-get-away-get-away-get-away."* Utterly bored, Catherine found herself snapping her fingers and making up silly verses to accompany the rhythm of the tires on the road. This bizarre behavior on the part of her mother caused Katie to dissolve into giggles, while other passengers merely rolled their eyes. Catherine chanted softly away, ignoring all the others.

> *The wheels of the bus go round and round,*
> *Takin' us far from Lancaster town.*
> *We packed our money, 'n we packed our bag.*

We're gonna zig an' we're gonna zag.
Where we goin'? I dunno.
I just know that we gotta go,
'Cause
Bad Daddy, made me do it, Oh,
Bad Daddy, made me do it, Oh,
Bad Daddy, made me do it, so
I just know that we gotta go. Hey!

A bearded man of undeterminable age leaned across the aisle toward Catherine. He was missing half his teeth. "Hey, honey, are you a songwriter or sumpin'?"

"No. Oh, no." Catherine sank down in her seat.

"Well, I usta play guitar. Y'know, we could make *beautiful* music together, what wit' your daddy been bad an' all that."

Catherine and Katie got off at the very next stop, although it was not their intended destination.

"No more singing, Mommy!" scolded Katie.

"Right," agreed her mother.

CHAPTER 9

Weary Travelers Rent a Nest

I T WAS MIDMORNING THREE DAYS later as the bus carrying Catherine and Katie rolled south down Highway 301. The vehicle lumbered past St. Petersburg and headed straight for Bradenton and Sarasota.

Catherine had been doing a lot of thinking. She had been told by various people along the way that Sarasota was the place to live in Florida. Good schools, beautiful beaches—much better place to raise a kid than Miami. For the moment, she knew she would have to put her career as a dance teacher on hold. She'd have to get money right away—waitressing, probably. But first, they'd have to find a place to stay. She had enough cash to cover food and apartment for two months at most, so she'd have to move fast. And of course, Katie would need to be enrolled in school, which was bound to start in a few weeks.

As they drove over the towering Skyway Bridge, a very nice lady let Catherine place a call from her personal cell phone. "I've got hundreds of minutes left, honey. Go ahead. Use it." A grateful

Catherine called her assistant, Larissa, in Lancaster in hopes that the girl would agree to take over the ballet studio.

Larissa had been one of Catherine's very first students at Dream Dancers. After she graduated from high school, Larissa moved on to New York City to continue her studies in modern dance. Within months, however, she came limping home, weeping and depressed, shattered by a disastrous urban romance. Horrified, her parents insisted that their only daughter stop running off. They had plenty of money. They could help, and they wanted her right here in Lancaster.

At her father's urging, Larissa began to nag Catherine to take her on as a business partner. Larissa's personal motive, however, was to reconnect with her high school boyfriend, for the handsome young man was looking more and more appealing by the minute.

So, yes, Larissa would love to take over Dream Dancers! As for coming up with money for Catherine, that was totally up to her dad. Unfortunately, he was in the hospital at the moment, doing battle with a leaky heart valve. Things were a little iffy, and Larissa would not talk to her father about Dream Dancers until he was out of the woods.

"Oh, honey, I'm so sorry. Yes, of course. Let him get well first. We can always talk later."

Larissa sounded worried. "I just hope and pray my dad gets better."

So do I, thought Catherine. *So do I.*

Catherine handed the cell phone back to her bus mate with copious thanks. She leaned back against the seat and stared out the dusty window and noticed the bus was entering the outskirts of Sarasota. It was not a pretty sight. US 301 did not cut through the tourist part of town. Instead, the highway ran past a string of gas stations, convenience stores, industrial parks, fast-food franchises, bars, strip clubs, palmists, and never-ending road reconstruction. Highway 301 was certainly no Rodeo Drive, but Catherine was certain the Gulf side of town would have a collection of restaurants.

There, she would have a better chance of finding an immediate job. Work was essential, for the little bit of money she had was rapidly evaporating.

The swaying of the bus had just lulled them back to sleep when the vehicle lurched into the Sarasota station. Catherine shook Katie awake, and the two of them stumbled down the stairs to claim their luggage. They could hardly get their legs to work. Three days on the road had proved to be a corrugating experience. Catherine felt as rumpled and scruffy as Highway 301, while Katie looked like an unkempt urchin.

"This is it, baby. As far as we go."

"Will Daddy find us?"

"Hope not."

"Me too. Hope he never, ever finds us. It is *over!*" Katie performed an emphatic parody of her mother's words, accompanied by the nod of a drama queen. It was not exactly a laughing matter, but Catherine was forced to stifle a giggle.

"Okay, Pickle. Let's go rent a nest."

"Cool!"

Catherine picked up the local paper and turned to the classified. A few minutes later, they were in a cab headed to look at a tiny garage apartment: $650 a month, utilities included, no pets.

"Do I count as a pet, Mommy?"

"Oh, usually, you do, you do, but not today. Today, you are a fine, upstanding young lady in desperate need of a bubble bath."

The garage sat behind a house owned by a cheerful Cuban lady by the name of Elba Martinez. She was round of face and full of body, and her jet-black hair had flecks of gray. Her small yellow house was crisply painted and had flowers sprinkled around the edges. The garage apartment had its own small yard, a giant oak, and a handmade wooden swing. Best of all, it was located right next to blocks and blocks of a long, thin park filled with benches and bike trails and tall shady trees.

Jackpot, thought Catherine.

Mrs. Martinez took them upstairs to see the apartment: two rooms, spotlessly scrubbed, filled with bright Mexican colors. "Perfect," said Catherine. "We'll take it!"

"Will you pay by the week or the month?" asked Mrs. Martinez.

"By the week until I get a job. But first, I've got to find a sitter."

Mrs. Martinez looked Katie up and down. "For this little cutie? I'd be glad to keep an eye on her until you settle in." Mrs. Martinez turned to Katie and comically wagged her finger. "You won't be able to pull anything fast on me, honey. I know everything there is to know about kids. Had six of my own."

Katie tilted her head and folded her arms. "Do you know how to bake cookies?"

"Got my PhD in cookies!"

"Cool! I love cookies." Katie gave Mrs. Martinez a cheerful hug. "Can I play on the swing?"

"It has your name on it!"

"Oh, this is the best place ever!" Katie scampered down the outside stairs and climbed up onto the big wooden seat. "Push me in the swing, Mommy. Push me in the swing!" Catherine dutifully followed her daughter down the stairs. Soon, the delighted child was soaring back and forth over the grass in giant arcs, the long bus ride from Lancaster utterly forgotten.

Catherine's thoughts were not so carefree. *How can I start another dance studio? If Larissa's father doesn't buy Dream Dancers, where else could I turn? Hiroki perhaps?*

CHAPTER 10

The Siesta Key Café

THINGS MOVED ALONG QUITE RAPIDLY. Catherine picked up a couple of bikes at the secondhand shop and then landed a job at the Siesta Key Café, a short ride from her new garage apartment. Sam Peacock was the owner, cook, and chief bottle washer. Because charm was not his strong suit, Sam counted on sweet-faced waitresses to keep customers marching through the door of his simple 1950s-style establishment. A retired paratrooper of Seminole descent, Sam was rough and gruff on the outside, but inside, he was pure marshmallow. Catherine felt on top of the job within the week.

She was behind the counter, busily filling coffeepots when Dr. Nicholas Kontos first entered her life. The Siesta Key Café was not one of Nick's regular stops. He usually bought his coffee out on Lido or Longboat, closer to his office at Gulf Marine Lab. Today, however, was different. Nick had just come in from sailing with friends on a sloop that was docked on Siesta.

The first thing Nick noticed about Catherine was her long, spectacular hair. Caught up in a tortoiseshell clip, it cascaded to her waist, reminding him of a Tahitian maiden he once met on a scuba-diving trip to the South Pacific. The second thing he noticed were Catherine's large sunburst earrings, which dangled and turned and caught the light. Striking in design, these earrings were made out of what appeared to be hammered gold, and they might well have belonged to an Aztec princess.

From the neck down, Catherine was dressed as a garden-variety coffee shop girl: checked dress, apron, Reeboks, and socks. Nothing much there of interest, except for the pin on her shoulder, which revealed her name.

Catherine went about her morning chores, barely stopping to look at her only customer. "Fresh coffee will be up in a few minutes," she called over her shoulder.

"Fine, Catherine. I'll wait." *I could sit here forever looking at you,* thought Nick, feeling frisky. *Classy name, pretty lady. Wonder if she scuba dives?*

Catherine walked into the kitchen, retrieved a box of sugar packets, and came back out to refill a series of small white containers. He started at her hands. *Good, she's not wearing a wedding ring.* He could not take his eyes off her, but she seemed not to notice.

Mrs. Martinez entered the door of the cafe followed by Katie, who burst into the establishment with a knapsack filled with drawing supplies. Nick turned to watch the exuberant little girl. "I won't be more than an hour, Catherine," called out Mrs. Martinez.

Catherine continued restocking the sugar bowls. "Take your time, Elba. It won't get busy until five."

After she set down her knapsack, Katie gave Mrs. Martinez an extravagant bear hug. "Remember, if the dentist says you gotta wear braces, get the pink rubber bands. My friend's big sister got blue ones, and boy, did she look yucky!"

Mrs. Martinez responded with a laugh "Right! See you in a little bit, honey. Take care of your momma." She waved and walked out of the café.

Catherine came out from behind the counter to kneel in front of Katie and give her a hug. "Hi, sweetie. Smart girl, you brought art supplies." After she took Katie by the hand, she led her to one of the booths in the back. "Sit right here, Pickle. What are you going to draw?"

Katie pondered the question. "I think … hmmm … I think—"

"Well, keep thinking. I've got to get back to work." Catherine turned and went back to the kitchen as Nick's eyes followed her.

Suddenly, Katie shrieked in excitement. "I've *got* it!" Nick turned to watch the child as she furiously began to work on her composition.

Catherine came out of the kitchen, and Nick took a stab at starting a conversation. "That's quite the little Picasso you have there."

"Mmm—" Catherine appeared distracted.

"I really liked drawing when I was a kid."

"Yes? Well, I'll get your coffee."

Well, talk about blowing me off, thought Nick. *She's sure not impressed with yours truly.*

Catherine poured a steaming mug and set it in front of Nick along with a spoon and a napkin. She then set down small bowls filled with thimbles of cream and packets of sugar. "May I get you anything else?"

"Apple pie maybe?"

"We have cherry or pecan. Those are the best."

"In that case, I'll have pecan." Catherine nodded, took a pie from the pie safe, and cut a fat slice as Nick looked on. She put a fork on the plate before she set it down in front of him.

"Thanks," he said, and she nodded.

Sam called out from the kitchen, "Catherine, could you come give me a hand?"

Catherine disappeared through the swinging door as Katie popped up at Nick's side, waving her drawing. "Hey, mister. Want to see my picture?"

"Sure." He took the paper and studied it. The drawing has one tall figure and one small figure. "Wow, you are good!"

Katie began proudly pointing out the finer points of her master work. "That's me! I'm the one in the ballerina suit. See, I'm wearing my gold necklace."

"Ah, it's got your name on it. And who's the other person?"

"That's my mommy. She's wearing her lee-o-tard. It's got a pink skirt."

"To go with the rubber bands on her braces?"

Katie started to giggle. "Ohhhhhhhh, my mommy doesn't wear braces."

"Too bad. Bet she'd look good in braces!"

"You're funny, mister!"

Sam emerged. He placed some clean cups under the counter and went back into the kitchen.

"That your daddy?" Nick asked.

"Nooooooo, that's Mommy's boss. He's a *nice* man. I've got a *baaaad* daddy!"

Nick was both startled and intrigued. "Oh?"

"Mommy and I are prob'ly not going to love Daddy anymore!"

Nick blinked. "I see."

Katie's voice dropped to a whisper, as if he was speaking to a conspirator. "We've been playing Zigzag."

"Really?"

Katie's whisper became even softer: "So Daddy can't find us."

"Ah—"

Then Katie abruptly returned to her normal speaking voice and announced, "Now I'm going to make a new drawing!"

"Go for it!"

Katie hopped to her booth and busily got back to work.

So that's it, thought Nick. *Her mother's gun shy. She's coming out of a bad relationship.*

Catherine backed through the swinging door, bearing another tray of mugs. As she set down the tray, Nick stood up and placed a couple of bills on the counter. For the first time, Catherine looked directly at him. "That is way too much!" she protested, pushing one of the bills back toward Nick.

He pushed the money back. "Keep it. You'll need it for art supplies."

Catherine appeared slightly flustered. "Oh … well, thank you."

Nick turned to Katie. "Keep up the great work, honey. You're going to be a famous artist someday."

Her head cocked to one side, Katie began coloring with a vengeance. When she saw her mother stare at the departing Nick, Katie abruptly stopped and spoke in a clear, bell-like voice, "He'd make a very good daddy."

Catherine made a face. "Shhhh, Katie … hush!" Embarrassed, she made herself busy as Sam backed through the swinging door.

Even with his back turned, Nick had heard what Katie had said. *The kid's on my side,* he thought, and he chuckled.

Later that afternoon, Nick took the helm of *Sandpiper*—one of the lab's three powerboats—and headed out to check traps. To get out to the Gulf of Mexico, he had to thread his craft through a series of keys and narrow islands that dotted Sarasota Bay just off the mainland.

As he neared Bird Key, he came upon a yellow sign protruding from the water that read, "Manatee Zone." Nick promptly dropped the boat down to "slow speed and minimum wake." No way was he going to injure one of the lumbering manatees inhabiting these tropical waters. Nick had fought hard for the safety of those endangered creatures. He had even helped write the Sarasota County Manatee Protection Plan, a plan which served to steer boats away from critical manatee habitats.

Besides, Nick secretly liked floating along in the slow zone. Here, he could take time to watch the sun move toward the horizon. Here, he was often treated to a glimpse of a manatee surfacing or the antics of a couple of dolphins. Nick liked the feel of the soft tropical air and luxuriated in a setting worthy of *National Geographic.*

Having passed peacefully through the manatee zone, Nick was

about to speed up when a water-skier went screaming by, hurling a great plume of water into the sky. The fast-moving boat was an inboard Donzi. Emblazoned across its stern were the words *Bad Daddy.*

"Well, how 'bout that!" exclaimed Nick. He thought of beautiful Catherine and her little Picasso and wondered what all that "bad daddy" stuff was about. He'd just have to get back to that Siesta Key coffee shop and find out.

CHAPTER 11

A Criminal Act

THE CLOCK AT THE SIESTA Key Café read almost eleven. Catherine wiped down counters as she waited for the last customer to depart. She was more than ready to go home. Most of the street had rolled up for the night, but lights were still on across the street where a small weekly newspaper called *The Pelican Press* was being put to bed. Catherine had gotten to know most of the newspaper staff. They often came in for lunch and sometimes for dinner when they were working late. Seeing that light on over at *Pelican* made her feel like she wasn't alone on the street.

Finally, her last customer paid his bill, left a small tip, and disappeared into the darkness. Catherine picked up his dishes and set them on the bus tray before she moved to lock up.

She was in process pulling the front door closed when a disheveled young man stuck his tattered boot in the door and blocked it. Catherine stared at his eyes as they darted around and felt a wave of fear. "I'm sorry. We're closed."

"Oh, no, you're not!" After he shoved the door open, the druggie brandished a gun. He was small and wiry with long, dirty hair. His pupils were noticeably dilated, and he moved with quick, agitated motions.

"Whoa!" Catherine backed up, hands in the air.

The man gestured toward the register with his gun. "Empty it!" When she didn't move fast enough, he jabbed her sharply with his gun. "Move it, lady. Move it!"

Catherine hands were shaking so hard that she had trouble opening the register. Finally, she succeeded and spread the currency out in a fan shape on the counter.

The druggie looked stoned and nervous. "You crazy? Put the money in a bag. Speed it *up!*" Catherine fumbled under the counter, found a brown paper lunch bag, and jammed all the bills inside. The intruder poked at her with the gun. "I'll take the chicken feed too—silver, no pennies." Catherine tried scooping up fistfuls of larger coins. She was so nervous she spilled them all over the floor.

"Shit!" screamed the man, and then he jumped over the counter. Still waving his gun, he shoved her aside and began awkwardly raking coins and bills into the brown paper bag. Her heart racing, Catherine backed away toward the safety of the street.

There was an elongated squeak as the kitchen door opened slowly to reveal a gun barrel pointed directly at the intruder. *Oh, God,* thought Catherine, and she dropped to the floor. Startled, the druggie turned, fired his own weapon at the attacking gun barrel, and missed it completely.

The kitchen gun went off with an earsplitting roar, and the shot lodged in the druggie's shoulder. Clutching the brown paper bag to his chest, the intruder stumbled toward the entrance of the cafe, shooting wildly. He shattered the big glass window and riddled the Sarasota Film Festival poster. There was a sharp ping as a bullet bounced off of a car parked on the street.

Sam burst through the kitchen door, his weapon in hand. "Catherine, are you okay?'

Catherine jumped to her feet. Her kneecaps were scraped, and her dignity had vanished. But that was about it. She looked nervously toward the entrance. "Is he gone?"

"Stay down. Stay down." With his gun drawn, Sam moved warily toward the front door. He emerged on the street only to see the druggie lurch off into the alley. Sam was about to give chase when he heard a voice he had once known as commander in chief.

"Christ, I sure hope this blood is fake!"

Looking down, Sam saw a man who looked like George W. Bush sitting on the sidewalk in a pile of shattered glass! The former president clutched his bleeding arm, which had been lightly grazed by a bullet. Sam could not believe his eyes. "Good Lord! Mr. President, are you hurt?"

"Of course I am, idiot! My shirt's turning red."

"Catherine!" Sam yelled. "Get out here! Bring towels. I'm calling 911!"

Sam raced back into the café as Catherine emerged from the door with a stack of kitchen towels. She, too, was flabbergasted by the identity of the victim. She sat on her haunches amid broken glass, pressing a towel on his bleeding arm. She was relieved to see that the injury appeared to be only a surface wound.

Having witnessed the commotion from his office window, a young reporter from the *Pelican Press* raced out from across the street, his camera at the ready. "Anybody hurt? What happened?" Suddenly, the reporter took a step back and gasped: "Oh, my God ... George W."

The man frowned and said, "See any Secret Service hanging around?"

The photographer looked around nervously. "No—"

"Well, I'm a fake—a George Bush impersonator. But this blood is mine, and it's real. I've been shot, you damned fool. Ow! Ow! It hurts!"

"Oh." There was a twinge of disappointment in the photographer's voice. For one brief moment, he had thought he was on the brink of catching a *really* big story.

The George W. look-alike stared down at his arm and saw that there wasn't much blood. "Huh. Doesn't look bad. Doesn't look deep. How's that for a piece of luck? Well, get off your asses and call 911."

"We've already called," Catherine assured him.

"Mind if I take your picture?" the reporter asked, hopeful to get a story out of it anyway.

Years of habit kicked in and the impersonator began mugging for the camera. "Sure. Catch me from the left. That's my most presidential side. And don't forget my pretty nurse."

Catherine recoiled. "No, no ... please, no pictures." She backed up through the café door as an ambulance arrived and attendants swarmed around the presidential lookalike.

A few days later, Luke Scanlon stopped at a convenience store in Lancaster to buy some Red Bull. He was paying the clerk with a ten-dollar bill when the cover photo on the *National Enquirer* caught his eye. He stared at the headline: "Bush 43 Falls Victim to Botched Robbery." In the large front page photograph, Catherine could clearly be seen in the background behind the fallen "president." Both Sarasota and the Siesta Key Café were named in the copy.

Luke motioned toward the paper rack. "I'll take one of those."

The clerk handed him a copy and a handful of change. As Luke stared at the photograph on the center front page, his jaw twitched and tightened.

CHAPTER 12

Calm Before the Storm

IT WAS EARLY IN THE evening one week later when Elba Martinez brought her beloved cat, Tigger, to Catherine's garage apartment. Elba was about to run off to Miami, where her first grandchild had just been born, a boy named Juan Patrick Martinez in honor of two grandfathers, one Irish, one Cuban.

During her landlord's absence, Catherine had arranged with Sam to work only day shifts so she would be home by supper. School would start in less than two weeks, and Catherine had signed her daughter up for the final stretch of summer camp. Mrs. Martinez's sister had been enlisted to cover any gaps in the schedule.

Katie had been assigned to supervise Tigger, a docile cat with a "lover boy" disposition. "I'll take good, *good* care of him—I promise," declared Katie. Catherine couldn't help but smile as she watched her child dragging this cuddly old cat around, stroking his prison-stripe fur.

Mrs. Martinez gave Tigger a good-bye scratch behind the ears.

"Remember, he loves TV, especially the Travel Channel. He likes to watch the lions and tigers."

It seemed as hard for Mrs. Martinez to leave Tigger as it would have been for Catherine to leave Katie. "Don't worry, Elba. Your kitty is in good hands. Go meet your grandbaby!"

"I can't wait to see that precious child. Give me a hug, Katie." It was another of those "mother bear" moments, but this time, a purring striped cat was included in the embrace.

Katie watched as the taillights faded in the distance. "Close the door, honey. We want Tigger to stay inside."

Katie did as she was told, pulling the door behind her. It closed, but not quite completely.

"Turn on Tigger's station, Mommy."

"Keep that kitty happy, huh, Pickle?"

"Very happy. See, he's purring!" Katie parked herself on the floor with Tigger on her lap, relentlessly stroking his silken fur. Catherine turned on the television and hunted for the Travel Channel. At the sound of Balinese music, Katie sat up tall and stared at the images she saw on the screen.

"Mommy, look—dancers like we saw in Ohio!"

Sure enough, Catherine could see two beautiful little Balinese girls who were eight or ten years of age, performing a Bumblebee Dance. Tightly encased in brilliant sarongs of pink and green, the children wore headdresses of glittering gold as they moved slowly across the screen. *I think I'll try to get Katie an outfit like that. Wouldn't she love it!*

They watched as the dancers executed intricate steps, knees bent, hips thrust back, their arms and fingers flowing through a cascade of graceful and sophisticated gestures. In a style unique to Balinese dance, their eyes moved sharply to the right and then sharply to the left while they always remained wide open. Throughout the entire dance, the girls never once blinked, maintaining slight smiles of incredible self-possession.

"Mommy, look at the sparkly golden hats!"

"Beautiful!"

The camera moved in for a close-up of the dancers' faces, eyes pulled abruptly to one side and small chins tilted. Swaths of eyeliner enhanced their dark eyes, while lips were painted a brilliant red.

Giggling, Katie rolled her eyes in imitation. "Look! I can do that! See, Mommy?"

Catherine laughed and said, "Indeed you can."

With that, Katie unceremoniously dumped Tigger on the floor, stood up, and announced, "I want to dance! I need a costume. Oh, Mommy, can you fix me up?"

Catherine loved playing games with her daughter. "Costume lady's on the case. Off with the shirt!" Katie tugged the garment over her head and stood barefoot in her shorts, impatiently awaiting her transformation. Her mother looked at the tiny gold necklace that glittered around her daughter's neck—a slender chain with the name Katie spelled out in gold letters. She remembered the day they had found it in a clothing shop. They'd gone in to buy a dress and had come out with a shiny necklace that Katie never, ever removed. *Good choice*, thought Catherine.

She took her new Hawaiian pareo out of the swimsuit drawer and wrapped Katie tightly round and round inside of it. She tucked and pinned and fashioned the brightly colored cloth into a sarong, and the child wiggled with excitement.

"The hat, Mommy. What about the hat?"

"Worry not, my darling." Catherine pulled a roll of silver foil off of the kitchen shelf.

Katie yelped, "That's not gold!"

"Silver, gold—what's the difference?"

"Silver, gold—what's the difference?" echoed Katie. Catherine was delighted with the wonderful game they were playing.

She doubled the foil and formed it into the shape of a crown. She cut more foil into strips, curling them with the back of the knife and looping them around the crown so that they dangled into a dramatic headdress of silver tentacles.

"Lipstick, Mommy. Those dancers were wearing lipstick."

As Catherine reached for her cosmetic bag, Tigger got up from his hiding place under the couch and sauntered over to check things out. His cat eyes stared as Catherine smudged Katie's eyes with purple and brushed her cheeks with soft pink.

"I loved to play 'Makeup' when I was your age, Katie."

Tigger began rubbing up against Catherine's hand. "Well, what do you think, Tig?" she asked. "Am I doing a great job?"

"He's purring, Mommy."

Tigger wheeled and walked haughtily away, striped tail waving. Catherine shrugged, "Well, so much for the cat's opinion. Now which color lipstick, baby?"

Katie jumped up and down. "The red! The red!"

"Simmer down, Katie." The child stopped bouncing and puckered her lips. Catherine carefully smudged her mouth with crimson and then leaned back to study the effect. "My, my, aren't you the Gilded Lily!"

"Oh, Mommy! You are *fun* to play with!"

Catherine laughed. "So are *you*, Pickle!" She reached over and gave Katie a hug.

On the television screen, the men of the Gamelan Orchestra could be seen hammering fiercely upon their instruments and filling the room with shimmering sound.

Fired up by the music, Katie pranced around, tossing her head and arching her feet. Once again, Catherine was amazed at her child's fascination with Balinese dance.

At 7:39 p.m. EST, their joyous world exploded.

CHAPTER 13

Nightmare

THE FRONT DOOR FLEW OPEN, and Luke Scanlon burst into the room, enraged and agitated. His dilated eyes darted around in an odd, jerky motion until they finally settled on Catherine, who froze in alarm.

"Why are you here?" she whispered.

Ignoring her, Luke slammed the door behind him. He shifted his gaze to Katie and stared at her with abject revulsion. What the hell was Catherine doing, painting the kid like a kewpie doll? Images of Aunt Cissy swirled through his head. *The ruby red lipstick, her eyes lined with black, her boobs spilling out of her top. His father gropin' like he was squeezin' melons—*

Luke looked at his child in horror. "You look like a friggin' sleaze queen!"

Katie ran to her mother. "We were just playing, weren't we, Mommy?"

Luke pulled Katie away and glared with disgust at Catherine. "You kidnap my kid, fix her up her like a floozy—"

Katie tried to wrench loose from her father's grasp. "I'm a *dancer*, Daddy! Please don't get mad."

With that, Luke went totally ballistic. "What are you up to, Catherine? The child's dressed like a *Spanish whore!* Are you selling her on the street?"

"Luke … now Luke, it's just a game," she said.

"Shut up!" Holding tightly to Katie's arm, Luke jerked off the silver foil headdress, crumpled it into a wad, and hurled it across the room. He ripped a dish towel off the rack, shoved it at the frightened child, and yelled, "Wipe off the damned paint!" Furious, he watched as his daughter swiped at her face with the towel, leaving great smears of bright red lipstick.

The clock in the kitchen read 7:41.

Catherine tried to pry Katie away from him. "I'll take her to the sink. I'll wash it all off—"

"Get your hands off my kid! I'm taking her home!" He dragged the tearful child toward the door.

"Mommy—"

"Luke, please. You've been drinking. We're not going."

"Who invited you, slut? God knows who you've been screwing!" His eyes narrowed as he shrieked: "You're nothing but a goddamn whore!"

"Luke—"

With the back of his hand, he struck Catherine to the floor, stunning her into silence.

Luke grabbed Katie and backed out the door, dragging her down the outside staircase. Ignoring her screams, he pulled her past the swing and onto the sidewalk, where he shoved her flailing and kicking into the front seat of his muddy green car.

He failed to notice that her foot had knocked the gearshift out of park.

Luke put his face up to his daughter's and glared. "Cut it out, Katie, or I'll beat the livin' crap outta you!" She cowered on the floor of the car, and he felt justified.

He climbed into the driver's seat and tried to start the engine again, but it would not turn over. As the starter growled and groaned, his face grew more and more purple. As she crawled up on the seat, Katie could see her mother scrambling down the stairs of the apartment. "Mommy!" she shrieked. The child attempted to open the passenger door, but Luke stopped her cold with a vicious slap.

As Catherine raced toward the car, Luke furiously kept grinding the starter. She had almost reached the vehicle when the engine kicked over. The car lurched forward, and he could hear her nails scratch at the trunk like a wild animal.

"You stupid bitch!" he screamed. The muddy green car squealed away, and the figure of his wife shrank in the rearview mirror.

The clock on the dashboard read 7:44.

Luke drove like a madman at three times the speed of light. Kneeling on the seat, Katie lurched back and forth, tears streaming down her face. "I hate you!" she cried.

"You're just like your fuckin' mother!" roared Luke, and he stomped down hard on the accelerator.

Catherine ran desperately in the wake of the vanishing car. It was hopeless, of course. The large red taillights had diminished into pinpoints, impossible to follow. The dark, empty street ran up the spine of a long slender park, now deserted. Catherine looked around frantically, but her cries went unheard.

"Help! I need help!" she sobbed.

The clock on the dashboard read 7:47.

As the speeding car emerged from the park, Katie dove for the door handle again and tugged on it with all her might. "I hate you! *I hate you!*" she screamed. Distracted, Luke swerved over the center line directly into the path of an oncoming car. Blinded by headlights, Luke jerked the wheel sharply to the right at the very same moment he reached out for Katie. In that pivotal move, his foot pressed down hard on the gas.

The force of the turn caused Katie's door to swing open. Luke made one last lunge for his daughter, but she pulled away. "I hate you!" she cried one more time. She slid though his grasp and vanished.

Luke screamed as the passenger door slammed against a road sign. His heart lurched in horror as the muddy green car spun out of control.

He heard a terrible grinding of metal as the car crashed through the guardrail and rolled over and over before finally coming to rest against a huge pine tree. The car landed on its side, engine smoking and wheels still spinning.

Everything turned black. Luke's world was over.

In the center of the park, Catherine froze dead in her tracks. The distant sounds of the crash pierced her heart like an arrow. "Oh, God," she whispered. Terror flooded her mind and body, and she began to shake uncontrollably. A wave of nausea washed over her, and she sank to her knees on the asphalt.

Not one car came by. Not one person was there to help.

That very evening, Nick Kontos had driven over to the Siesta Key Café in hopes that he might find the lovely Miss Catherine working behind the counter. No luck. Another waitress was on duty. She informed Nick that for the moment, Catherine was scheduled to work the day shift. "Well, guess I'll be back for lunch," said Nick. He was feeling deflated. His only mission had been to find Catherine. Still, it was suppertime, and the food looked okay, so he ordered the dinner special: chicken pot pie with mashed potatoes and gravy.

The street was deserted as he headed for home, pondering his wasted evening. *Lunch, huh? Well, it's a bit of a drive, but I'll make it happen.*

It was 7:47. He had approaching Siesta Key Park when the headlights of an oncoming car appeared and began weaving toward him like a sidewinder. Suddenly, the lights lurched over the center line and became enormous. Nick spun his car onto the shoulder, and the two vehicles shot past each other, barely missing a head-on collision. Nick jumped out of his car in time to see the offending car veer right, hurtle over the guardrail, and disappear from sight amid the earsplitting sounds of crushing metal.

Oh, Christ! Nick ran back along the road, heart racing. He peered over the broken rail and was shocked at the chaos below him. He flipped open his cell phone and dialed 911.

"Nick Kontos here. Terrible wreck, possibly fatal. South of Siesta Bridge outside the park." He snapped the phone shut, took a deep breath, and looked around to see what he could do.

When he spotted a tiny figure crumpled by the side of the road, Nick ran to it. Kneeling down, he gasped in recognition. *Oh, my God, it's the little Picasso!* To his utter dismay, blood was pouring out of a gaping hole in her side. He desperately tried to apply pressure; however, the hole was too large, and her blood kept seeping through his fingers.

The child's eyes fluttered open, and she stared at Nick as the color drained from her face. "My daddy doesn't love me anymore. My name is Katie. Will you take care of me?"

"Sure, honey. Yes— Yes—"

Her voice was barely a whisper. "And my mommy?"

Nick fought to hold back tears. "Of course, Katie. Whatever you want."

Nick tried helplessly to stem the flow of blood as it ebbed from her body. Katie's voice grew smaller as the pool of blood became larger.

"Mommy, Mommy, that really nice man is here—"

"Please, God. Let Katie live," whispered Nick, desperate to save her.

"Push me in the swing, Mister. Higher—" He heard her voice trail off. Her eyes closed, and she was still.

Stunned, Nick found himself kneeling in her pool of blood. Suddenly, he remembered that there had to be a driver. Reluctantly, he turned his attention to the smoking wreck. A man's boneless body lay motionless outside the car, as limp as a sack of flour. Nick knew in an instant the man was dead.

The clock in his cell phone read 7:51.

In barely twelve minutes, Catherine Scanlon's world had been shattered.

CHAPTER 14

A World in Upheaval

POLICE CARS AND AMBULANCES ARRIVED, sirens blaring. Nick turned away, not wanting to watch as grim-faced medics tried to resuscitate Katie. He was standing in the dark by his car, arms folded, when a creature flew past his face. Startled, Nick brushed it away. *Must be a bat*, he thought. As it looped past the ambulance and disappeared in the trees, there was an almost subliminal flash of yellow.

A police officer approached, a longtime acquaintance. "Hello, Nick."

"Hi, Andrew."

"What a lousy, rotten mess here! Are you hurt?"

"No, I'm okay. Just a bit shaken."

"I would think so." Andrew took out his notebook and pen. "Can you tell me what happened?" As he dug for his pen, Andrew paused. From the corner of his eye, he could see a slender woman on the road moving slowly toward them as if in a trance. "Uh-oh. Who's that?"

Nick knew who it was in a moment. "It's the child's mother."

"Oh, I hate this." With a sigh, the policeman put his notebook and pen away and went toward Catherine. Nick followed a few steps behind, unsure of what action to take.

Catherine moved like a sleepwalker toward the broken guardrail. There, she stopped and gazed down at the wreckage of the car. An ambulance attendant was standing near Luke, who laid motionless, glazed eyes frozen and staring upward. "Is he dead?" she asked, her voice completely devoid of emotion. The ambulance attendant nodded. "And my daughter?" The man motioned over to the side of the road, where she saw other attendants bending over Katie's lifeless body. Catherine ran toward them and pushed them aside.

When she saw Katie, she went into an almost catatonic shock. Her hands covered her face as she backed away in horror. There were no tears. She did not cry. Instead, she let out a low, primal groan as though her life has been swept away.

Andrew had caught up with her by then and tried to comfort her. Nick remained in the background, not knowing the best thing to do. His thoughts centered on the beautiful little girl who had once shown him her drawing at the coffee shop. His mind replayed her final words: *Will you take care of me? And my mommy?*

Nick ran his hand through his hair as he paced back and forth. A glint on the pavement caught his eye. It was the tiny gold necklace with the word Katie on it. *Surely, her mother will want that,* he thought, and he picked up the necklace and slipped it into his pocket for safekeeping.

The police had procedures for situations like this, and Andrew had questions he needed to ask. "I am so very sorry, ma'am," he stammered, clearly embarrassed. "But ... well, I need to ask a few questions. Could you identify—"

Catherine's voice was flat and colorless. "My husband ... and my child."

Andrew scribbled in his notebook. "And your name, ma'am?"

"I ... I'm Catherine Scanlon. My husband is ... was Luke Scanlon. Our daughter, Katie."

"Was there a domestic problem?"

"My husband became violent when he drank. We ran away from him a month ago, but tonight, he found us. And he took Katie."

Andrew frowned. "Do you come from around here?"

Catherine shook her head. "No, we ran away from Ohio. Sarasota seemed so far. I thought we'd be safe."

Andrew continued gathering information as ambulance attendants put bodies on stretchers to prepare for the trip to the morgue. Nick stood a short distance away, hoping somehow to be of help. As the tow truck arrived, Andrew snapped shut his notebook and sighed. Here came the part all policemen hated.

"Mrs. Scanlon, in cases like this, there have to be autopsies."

"Oh, God—"

"Then maybe Brown's Funeral Home or Chandlers. Both are small, family-run businesses, reputable. They won't— Well, they'll be fair."

"Thank you."

"Is there someone to call? A clergyman? A sister? A friend?"

Catherine shook her head. "No, there is no one." For the first time, tears started to stream down her face.

Stunned by Catherine's loneliness, Nick finally stepped forward. "Please. Let me be of help."

"Mrs. Scanlon? This is Dr. Nicholas Kontos. He's well known in the community." Catherine nodded, almost imperceptibly.

"Andrew, I'll do all I can. I'll take her wherever she needs to go."

"Thanks," said Andrew.

How can I live without Katie? thought Catherine. *I can't do this alone.* She allowed Nick to put a protective arm around her and lead her to his car.

A flash of color appeared in the woods on the far side of the road. It took the form of Katie. She was dressed in a Balinese costume of hot pink and green with a headdress of glittering gold. She stood quietly beneath a tree with a yellow bird perched on her shoulder.

Mommy, I'm here. I'm right here beside you.

CHAPTER 15

A Shattered Heart Seeks Compassion

Once inside the car, Nick saw that tears were falling down Catherine's face. He struggled for words, which, when they came, seemed utterly trite. "It's all right. Let it out. Go ahead and cry." He felt helpless.

He hesitated for a moment. Then instinct overwhelmed him, and he took Catherine into his arms, holding her and rocking her in a primal gesture of compassion. "Oh, Catherine, how terrible this must be for you. That beautiful child— I am so very, very sorry." Through it all, Nick fought tears of his own.

They sat in the car by the side of the road for a long, long time, Nick rocking her and stroking her long dark hair. Slowly, slowly, Catherine's tears subsided, and she started to talk. At first, her words were scattered, her voice muffled. "My husband swore that he'd take Katie from me. He was a drunk, maybe even an addict. I don't know how our lives went so berserk."

Then she began to talk of her treasured little girl. She spoke in random bits of memory, to which Nick could only listen. She told of birthday parties and walks to the park. She told of reading books and riding bikes and making cupcakes together, tales that made it seem like her daughter still lived upon this earth. "Katie was filled with light," said Catherine. "She loved dancing and singing and dressing up. She loved Tigger the cat and her canary and—" Her voice broke off. "I think I'd better go home."

"I'll take you," said Nick. He started the car. "Which way do I go?"

"Straight ahead through the park. Not far. Six blocks maybe."

They pulled up in front of the apartment. Mrs. Martinez's cat sat at the top of the flight of steps, silhouetted against the living room lights. The door had been left wide open, and the television was on, tuned to a piano concert on PBS.

"Is that Tigger?"

Catherine nodded.

Nick parked the car, and they moved up the stairs. The cat greeted them by rubbing against their ankles. "Good boy. You stayed home," said Catherine. Nick watched as she picked up the cat and buried her face in his fur. Suddenly a paw caught in her large gold earring. "Ouch!" After she unhooked the paw, she set Tigger back down as her earring dangled precariously.

"Need help?" asked Nick.

"I've got it." Catherine refastened the wayward piece of jewelry. The earring was really quite remarkable, a large wide hoop, flat and hammered, with small added sunburst shapes that looked as if they had been crocheted out of golden ribbon. "Katie always liked these best," she said.

"They're beautiful," said Nick.

Nick paused at the door, wondering whether or not he should enter. "Please. I don't think I could stand being alone," said Catherine, and he nodded. With the cat leading the way, they stepped into the apartment. On the television, a young composer was seen playing a haunting melody, a simple piano solo of heartbreaking beauty.

Catherine's tears welled up again as she came upon the framed picture of Katie lying on the floor, its glass shattered. Nick watched as she closed the frame and set it carefully on the table.

The room was in disarray. The contents of a makeup box were strewn across the floor. Catherine appeared dazed as she picked up the scattered objects, setting them in neat rows on the kitchen counter. The heartrending piano piece came to an end, and Nick turned off the television.

Catherine reached down to retrieve the kitchen towel her daughter had used to wipe off the offending makeup. As she buried her face in the cloth, her shoulders began to shake. Nick put his arm around her and led her to the couch, where he held her and gently stroked her silken hair. As her sobbing grew, he cradled her as if she was a child, letting her cry upon his shoulder.

"Don't go," she whispered.

"I won't."

He rocked her back and forth for a long, long time until finally her weeping subsided.

"Come with me," she said. He looked at her in surprise. She took his hand and led him to her bed, where they stretched out on the quilt, fully clothed. Nick stayed by her side, stroking her hair, talking gently to her, his heart breaking almost as much as hers. Catherine's eyes remained wide open, and her dark hair spilled across the pillow, a frame for her golden earrings. A church bell struck the hour, and in what seemed like no time at all, it struck again.

By the middle of the night, a tropical storm had gathered. Rain came pouring down, pounding the old tin roof with its wetness and creating the sound of pure white.

Of all the many women Nick had known, not one had affected him like this. As Nick continued to hold and comfort her, his universe became compressed into one tiny room where only two people existed.

"No one has ever been so kind to me before," she whispered. "Why are you being so caring?"

"How could I not be," he said, and the words came from his heart.

As the hours passed, Catherine began to slowly respond to Nick's extraordinary gentleness. Things started to build, and Nick pulled back, uncertain of the road he should travel. Catherine touched his arm, and her eyes looked deep into his.

"Make everything go away," she murmured.

"Catherine, are you sure?"

She did not answer. Instead, she took his face in her hands, pulled it close up to hers, and kissed him.

This can't be the right thing to do, thought Nick. But it was.

He was so tuned into her by now that he had but one goal, to express caring and human contact. Nick wanted only to bring beauty back into Catherine's shattered life. His single desire was to erase the terrible anger and tragedy she had experienced. In that moment, he became an artist-lover capable of expressing things he never knew existed.

They spent the night entwined in each other's arms. The sounds of the warm summer rain continued to surround them, while an occasional flash of lightning illuminated their faces.

It was dawn when Nick dozed off, exhausted. Was it a memory? Was it a dream? He saw Katie's face and heard her say, "Push me in the swing—"

Nick sat bolt upright to find Catherine standing at the window, arms folded, staring down at the empty swing.

He got up from the bed to join her. Together, they gazed at the vacant swing, which was swaying slowly back and forth. He reached out to put his arm around her shoulder, but she stiffened abruptly and pulled away.

Suddenly, she wheeled to confront him. "What the hell are we doing? I want you to go."

Nick appeared stunned. "Catherine—"

Her voice was pure ice. "We made a terrible mistake."

His face looked shocked. "I thought you needed me."

"You took advantage. You thought I was vulnerable. You're just like every other man I've ever known. I want you to get out!"

Nick angrily protested, "I'm not like that! You know nothing about me."

"I don't *want* to know anything about you. It's better if I don't even know your name."

"It's Nicholas. Nicholas Kon—" Catherine pressed her hand hard against his mouth, cutting him off.

"No names! I don't want to see you. I don't want to hear from you. I will *never* think of you again!"

Nick looked bewildered. He began pulling on his clothes as words poured from his mouth. "Look, I was trying to help. I made a mistake. When you're ready—a month, a year, whatever—I'll come to you. We'll start over again at the beginning."

Catherine turned away, shaking her head. "For me, there will be no more beginnings. Just go!"

Nick grabbed for his jacket and moved toward the door. Then he turned to look back, reaching for something to say. "Catherine, you're unlike any woman I have ever known. I've got to see you again."

Catherine shook her head, her voice flat and colorless. "No. Never. Get out. This night has been erased!"

Nick left the apartment, slamming the door behind him. He felt spent and depressed, as if he had done something cruel and stupid. As he moved down the wooden stairs, he could feel Catherine's eyes staring at him from the upstairs window. Looking back, his eyes caught hers, and she yanked the curtain closed.

Nick climbed reluctantly into his car. As he looked in the rearview mirror, he thought he saw the ghostly figure of Katie sitting in the swing. Her eyes and lips were boldly painted, and her headdress was made of glittering gold. She was wrapped in the beautiful costume of a Balinese dancer.

Startled, Nick turned abruptly around. The vision of Katie had vanished. *Oh, great! Now I'm hallucinating!* Dejected, he turned the key in the ignition and drove slowly away.

⁓

It was three days later when Nick arrived at the graveyard. The somber sounds of the church bells rang out as Luke's large brown coffin and Katie's small white coffin were about to be lowered into the ground. There were only a handful of mourners: Sam from the diner, Andrew the policeman, Mrs. Martinez, Catherine, the priest, and Nick, who stood back toward the edge of the group. A few flowers had been placed near the gravesites. Through it all, Catherine never once glanced toward Nick.

Father John said a few homilies and ended with these words: "We do not know why God has chosen to take this troubled father and this precious child, but we must search our hearts for forgiveness. Let us pray."

The poetry of the Lord's Prayer rang out over the graveyard. "Our Father, who art in heaven, hallowed be thy name—"

As the prayer continued, a small yellow bird began to warble melodiously. He perched on a tree branch above the graves, ruffling his feathers and singing with all his might. Catherine looked up at the little bird. "Mr. Sunshine," she whispered, and her eyes filled with tears.

When the service was over, Nick attempted to speak with Catherine, but detached and remote, she turned away.

Oh, God, Catherine. You were too broken, too vulnerable. I should never have crossed that line. What can I do to erase that?

He stepped back, crushed, as Catherine moved toward the funeral car that carried her away.

CHAPTER 16

Some Things One Never Forgets

IT WAS MONDAY THREE DAYS later when Nick pulled into his parking place in front of Gulf Marine Laboratory. It was early, and the parking lot was empty, except for the car belonging to Marty, his assistant.

Nick had not felt like coming in to work. The death of Katie had profoundly disturbed him. To make matters worse, he had become obsessed with memories of Catherine, turning over and over in his mind the ways he might break through to her. One thing was sure: he had to find a way to see her again.

Nick understood Catherine's anger. The death of Katie was so horrific that it was only natural for her to strike out at anything and everything.

It was my fault, of course, thought Nick. *I should have protected her. I was traumatized too in a way, but nothing like the agony she was going through. What I felt was compassion, not lust. I didn't mean to take advantage, but I guess you could read it that way.*

He should have thought of all that earlier, of course, but the fact was … he hadn't.

Oh, God, I totally messed up. I meant Catherine no harm. I felt overwhelmed by the need to comfort her. Things just got away from us. What can I do about that now? Wait a while maybe … until her heart starts to heal. Perhaps then I could approach her.

Nick entered Gulf Marine's swinging doors, took the elevator up to the second floor, and headed for his office. The lab was a plain, workhorse building with lots of elephant gray filing cabinets and not much in the way of artwork. Nick didn't care. He never paid much attention to the building anyway. The research they did was the stuff that mattered.

Nick stood at his desk, rifling through the mail when his assistant walked in carrying a small stack of papers. Marty was one of Nick's favorite dive buddies. He was also a notorious party animal. *Hell, so was I at twenty-seven,* thought Nick. *He's shorter than I am, but muscular and good-looking, so the ladies really go for him. Well … that's his problem, not mine.*

"Hi, Marty. Have a good weekend?"

"Super-spectacular!"

"Went fishing, huh?"

"Caught me a mermaid."

"Good man!"

Nick sat down behind his desk and motioned to Marty to take the other chair. "Okay, let's get down to business. That grant application—is it finished?"

"Here's where I am." Marty pushed papers across the desk. "I'm wrestling with the part about overfishing. Our stats are not up to date."

"I can fix that. Hearst Research Station is doing studies off Catalina Island. Call Bonnie and see what she's got. If that doesn't work, call Scripps. Jerry Butler's the man over there. We've got to get cracking!"

Marty peered blearily down at his diver's watch. "Hey, let me wake up first, boss. It's 5:00 a.m. in California. They're still out drinking and dancing."

Nick frowned. "Don't fool around with this, Marty. I need to get this application done and off my desk. I want to concentrate on another project." *If indeed you can call Catherine a project.*

Marty made a face. "Boy, you're sure acting strange, boss. Maybe it's time you caught a mermaid of your own." He wandered out of the room in search of coffee.

Oh, I've found my mermaid all right, thought Nick. *Problem is she won't have anything to do with me.*

Nick made a feeble effort to skim through the papers Marty had left behind, but his mind kept drifting back to the night Katie had died in his arms. He had seen her only once before her heartbreaking death, yet he was amazed at the impact she had had upon his life. There was something especially awful about the demise of a child.

Nick thought of his parents and the tragedy of his little sister, Meredith. Spinal meningitis had taken her when she was only eight. His parents had taken her off on an adventure trip through the jungles of Brazil. Three weeks later, they came back on the plane with Meredith in a coffin. Her shocking death had so shattered Nick that he took a year off from university to get past his depression. Fact was his mother never truly recovered from the loss.

Struggling to push these memories aside, Nick turned his mind to his night with Catherine. He had visions of her sad, lovely face, earrings glinting against swaths of dark hair. He could almost hear the beautiful melody that was playing that night, filling his heart. He remembered the rain pouring down and the softness of her voice and his need to hold her in his arms.

The alarm went off in his head, screeching like a banshee. *Oh, God, how crass! I sound worse than a cheap dime novel! Knock it off, man. Go out in the boat or something.*

A familiar voice interrupted. "Well, if it isn't the brilliant, the sexy, the fabulous Dr. Kontos!"

Nick turned to face Dr. Alexandra Knight. She stood in the doorway, dressed in her usual hottie attire—high heels and jeans with something flimsy on the top. Nick was in no mood to deal with her. He just wasn't up to her games.

Lexi looked faintly exasperated. "Well, talk about a lukewarm reception. How about a hug for the queen of frequent fliers?"

"Oh, sure. Welcome back!" Nick gave her a perfunctory embrace. "So ... how did it go in the islands?"

"I learned you're the best-looking marine biologist on the planet. I learned we have an incredible operation here and that you and I are a team extraordinaire. I also learned that people are starving, the reefs are crumbling, and fish are disappearing at an alarming rate."

"Sorry I asked. Same old stuff, huh?"

Lexi was on a roll. She paced back and forth, pontificating, and the sound of her stilettos hitting the wooden floor provided auditory exclamation points. "Daddy's right. We need Washington behind us! We need the United Nations behind us! We need grants! We need money! We need manpower!"

"I need to check the traps for specimens."

"Ah, Mr. Pragmatic. Right now? This very second?"

"Yep."

"May I come along?"

Nick shrugged. "Why not? Your father bought us the boat."

By 10:00 a.m., the Gulf Marine speedboat, which was named *Sandpiper*, had entered the Gulf of Mexico. Nick had smoothed the transition from bay to gulf by going under the bridge that linked Lido to Longboat. He changed into long baggy swim shorts, a T-shirt, and a hat, while Lexi sported an orange bikini, which, in Nick's opinion, was much too provocative for this professional occasion. The motor made a great deal of noise. *Good,* thought Nick. *I don't have to bother with conversation.* Periodically, he stopped the boat to check traps and remove occasional creatures, transferring them to a small marine aquarium on board.

Lexi said nothing at first and Nick could feel her irritation. He knew full well that she hated to be ignored. *Too bad, honey. That's just the way it is.*

The boat came to another stop. Nick picked up the grapple and hauled in the trap. From the corner of his eye, he saw Lexi pull a bikini strap off her shoulder, revealing a naked breast. Nick swiveled around to find his colleague, Dr. Alexandra Knight, staring ever-so-innocently out to sea and looking completely disheveled.

"Hey, Lexi, you're falling apart," he said cheerfully and kept right on unloading the trap.

"Oops," she exclaimed, readjusting her top.

Nick fired up the *Sandpiper* as if nothing had happened. He chose to ignore Lexi's fierce look of determination.

When Nick was driving home after work, the same haunting melody he had heard in Catherine's apartment came on the car radio. Performed on the piano without any words, the piece was reminiscent of an etude by Chopin, and touched both his heart and his memory. Nick turned up the volume and once again became lost in a collage of flashbacks about his extraordinary encounter with Catherine.

He parked the car in the garage and waited for the music to end before he entered his house, a simple cypress home he'd done nothing to make homey, surrounded by out-of-control vegetation.

Once inside, he turned up the air conditioner, threw his jacket on the chair, and poured himself a club soda. When he checked his messages, he found nothing of consequence. Good! He didn't want to talk to anybody anyway.

Nick grabbed the remote, unbuttoned his shirt, and settled down to watch the evening news. As he sprawled in the chair, his jacket slid to the floor in a heap. When he got up to retrieve it, Nick saw that a small, broken chain had fallen out of the pocket. Puzzled, he picked it up and saw the name Katie hanging from the center of the chain. *Damn—I'd completely forgotten.*

The necklace glinted in the palm of his hand. As he stared at it, his thoughts turned to his last moments with Katie. He recalled his feeling of sick helplessness as her blood seeped through his fingers, and he heard her dying words: *My daddy doesn't love me anymore. Will you take care of me ... and my mommy?*

As he spilled the gold chain back and forth in his hands, the specter of Katie seemed to slowly materialize in the window behind him. She was wearing a Balinese costume.

Nick could feel her presence. When he turned, he saw her, and his breathing stopped. *Oh, Lord—*

On the other side of the window glass, Katie smiled serenely, and her childish voice reverberated in his heart, "Please ... take my necklace to my mommy."

With that, the apparition faded. An astonished Nick was left to wonder, *Have I gone completely mad? And why would Katie be dressed like that?*

CHAPTER 17

Moving Along

THE NEXT DAY, NICK CLIMBED the stairs to Catherine's garage apartment. The door to the apartment was open, and the rooms had been stripped of her belongings. All that remained of her brief residency was a small pile of trash.

A handyman was up on a ladder, installing new lightbulbs. A cigarette dangled out of his mouth, spilling ashes all over his paint-splattered overalls. "Excuse me. Is Mrs. Scanlon around?" asked Nick.

The man climbed down the ladder, took the cigarette out of his mouth, and spoke in a gravelly voice: "She's moved on, poor lady."

"Any idea where she went?"

The workman shook his head. "Nope. Didn't leave no address."

Nick felt the wind knocked from his sails. He looked around the empty room, furtively hunting for hints to Catherine's whereabouts.

The workman stubbed his cigarette out in an empty can. "You a friend of hers?"

"Yes."

The man gestured toward the pile of trash. "She forgot that photo disk over there … and that wood jewelry box. I don't have no place to send them."

"I'll see that she gets them."

"Oh, and I found a kid's drawing. She might want it, seeing as the kid … well, you know."

Nick nodded. He picked up drawing and studied it. It was the very same one that Katie had shown him in the coffee shop. Nick sighed and then carefully rolled it up. "Got a rubber band?"

The man dug through his overall pockets and fished out a thin ring of rubber. He handed it to Nick, who slipped it over the rolled-up drawing.

After retrieving the photo disk and the jewelry box, Nick lingered, reluctant to leave. He scanned the room, stalling, looking for any shred of information that somehow might lead him to Catherine. He checked out the rest of the trash, but the only object of possible interest was a back issue of *Yoga Journal*. "May I take this?"

"Why not? It's headed for the recycle bin."

"Thanks."

The man gave a nod, lit another cigarette, and climbed back up the ladder. For one last time, Nick surveyed the room. Satisfied he had not overlooked any clues, he picked up his treasures and said good-bye. As he walked down the outside stairs, he passed the tree. In his mind, he could hear Katie's words: *Push me in the swing, mister. Push me in the swing—*

With his free hand, Nick sent the wooden swing soaring.

CHAPTER 18

Return to Lancaster

CATHERINE'S FLIGHT HAD NOT GONE well. The man seated next to her reminded her dimly of someone she knew.

Who was it? she wondered. *Who was it?*

And then she remembered. He looked like the man at the accident, the man who had driven her home. A wave of guilt washed over her. *They had made love. On the very night Katie was killed. How could they both have been so callous?* She pushed away thoughts of that night. The encounter should never have happened, and she was determined never to think of it again.

Turning away from her seatmate, she stared out the window of the plane. The clouds were gray and heavy just like her heart.

At the Lancaster airport, she quickly found a taxi and gave the address of the place that had once been her home, the house in which Katie had been born.

The cab moved along familiar streets, and Catherine's mind was flooded with memories.

There was the restaurant where Luke had proposed. Was it just seven years ago? How nice he had seemed at the time, how attentive. There wasn't a glimmer of the monster he would one day become. How could I have known? But I should have.

Tears started to flow, and Catherine could not restrain them. The driver looked in the mirror and frowned. "Hey, lady, are you all right?"

Her nod was almost imperceptible. She dabbed at her eyes with a Kleenex until the tears subsided.

I pushed Katie's stroller down this very street. And there—over there—was the park where Katie learned to ride a bike.

As the cab moved past the library, Catherine thought of the book they had found there on Bali. *Katie begged me to read it to her as soon as we got home, and I did. Oh, I'm so very glad I did.*

She thought of the hours Katie had spent studying photographs in the book. Her daughter had been captivated by the young Balinese dancers, all gloriously wrapped in brilliantly colored cloth. She had loved their elaborate makeup and their bright golden hats. "I want to dance like those pretty girls," Katie had cried. "I want to wear those sparkly dresses. May we go there someday, Mommy?"

On that long ago day, Catherine had smiled and nodded. "This is an amazing world. Anything's possible. Just keep on dreaming—"

The poignant memories caused tears to well up once again. *How desperately I miss you, Katie. You were my ray of light. I never thought I'd lose you, especially in such a pointless, evil way.*

As if in answer to her thoughts, Catherine imagined she heard words once spoken by Katie in a faraway bus station: *You haven't lost me, Mommy. I'm right here beside you.*

Catherine wept. *Oh, God, if only that were true—*

The sun had just dipped below the horizon when the taxi pulled up in front of a small white house. The windows were dark, and the lawn looked shaggy and unkempt.

"Is this the place?" asked the driver.

"Yes." Catherine paid the man and got out of the cab. Even in the evening light, she knew that her eyes looked puffy.

"Ma'am, are you sure you're okay? Do you want me to call someone for you?"

"No, thank you. I'll be fine."

"Well, let me carry your bag to the top of the stairs."

"I'd appreciate that."

Catherine took a deep breath and climbed toward the door. *The last time I was here, it was with Katie.*

She turned the key in the lock and entered. Three weeks' worth of mail had fallen through the mail slot, forcing her to step over a pile of unopened bills and catalogs. The rooms were dark and musty, unwashed dishes dumped in the sink, Luke's dirty laundry piled in front of the washer. When Catherine turned on the light, she could see that the trash was filled with empty liquor bottles. One lone cockroach scuttled across the floor.

She did not react to the mess she confronted. She was still too much in shock. Her mind stayed stuck on ten small words: *The last time I was here, it was with Katie.*

A thousand miles to the south, Nick sat at his kitchen table, drinking his after-dinner cup of coffee. Katie's drawing was displayed on the refrigerator behind him, while the small wooden box had been placed on the counter with the gold Katie necklace coiled safely inside. There, too, was a clipping from last Sunday's paper: "Father and Daughter Killed in Wreck."

As he ran his finger down the newsprint, Nick stopped at the words *Lancaster, Ohio*. He picked up the phone and dialed the operator. "Please connect me with the Luke Scanlon residence in Lancaster. The name is spelled S-C-A-N-L-O-N. Yes … Lancaster, Ohio."

In Catherine's house, a telephone began to ring. She turned to stare at the phone but made no move to answer. Instead, she sorted through a cluster of keys and found the one that fit the bottom desk drawer. After she turned the key in the lock, she rummaged through the drawer and unearthed a bankbook. She studied the check register and frowned, then put the bankbook in her purse.

Though it all, the phone never stopped ringing. Catherine ignored it. She returned to the drawer and fished out her American passport. It had been issued when she was still single, before Luke had even entered her life. She'd never bothered to update the information.

When she flipped open the dark blue cover, she checked the expiration date. *I'm in luck. It's still in effect.* The picture on the inside page showed a young woman smiling, a girl by the name of Catherine Elizabeth Donovan. She was twenty-four years of age, single, with hair that was cropped in a pixie cut.

Catherine could hardly recognize herself. The person in that photograph looked like a total stranger. *Was I ever that young? Was I ever that happy?* She tried to remember, but she simply could not.

After an epic number of rings, the phone finally stopped. Catherine never even looked up. Instead, she entered the tiny bathroom, propped her passport open on the sink, and studied the head shot of a woman she barely remembered. Then—carefully removing her treasured earrings—she placed them on the counter and pulled a pair of silver scissors from a crowded drawer.

For several long moments, she studied her reflection in the mirror. Then—carefully and methodically—she began to cut away at her long tresses, clipping them strand by strand, snipping them close to the scalp. As she worked, she spoke aloud to herself with great deliberation, and the snap of the scissors orchestrated her words.

"Catherine . . . Elizabeth . . . Donovan . . ." Silver blades flashed in the mirror. "Known as Elizabeth . . ." Broad swaths of hair cascaded to the floor. "Single . . . American . . . headed for a new life on the island of Bali."

As the last strand fell, Catherine defiantly lifted her chin. A tangle of chocolate brown hair now lay in a swirl at her feet. Luke's terrible betrayal, the horror of her daughter's last night on earth, her foolish indiscretion—these things had all been cut away and need never be thought of again.

With Katie in her heart, she would go to Bali. There she would begin anew.

As Catherine slowly put her earrings back on, she remembered words Katie once said in that very same room. *I love those earrings, Mommy. They make you look so pretty.*

Catherine fought back tears. *I'll always wear them, Pickle, 'cause they make me think of you.*

The phone started to ring once again, but Catherine made no attempt to silence it.

The following day, Nick handed Catherine's forgotten photo disk to the photo lab technician at Walgreen's. "How many prints?" the technician asked.

"Two each. Four-by-six."

"They'll be ready in an hour."

"I'll be back. Thanks."

CHAPTER 19

New Directions

A NEWLY SHORN CATHERINE SPENT SEVERAL days clearing the Lancaster house of all family belongings. She also took on the tedious task of getting financial matters in order. The small amount of insurance money coming to her would barely cover bills she had charged for the funeral. Larissa's father had agreed to buy out her interest in the ballet school, and he would pay for it in three annual installments. That was all Catherine would have, but it was enough. She knew how to be careful with money, and besides, buying things no longer seemed important.

It felt right to be heading for Bali. She and Katie had dreamed of going there ever since they had watched those beautiful child dancers. It felt like Katie would want her to go. It felt like the place to make a new beginning.

Catherine pulled a tattered magazine article out of her purse: "Restore Your Soul in Beautiful Bali." It had been clipped from a publication called *Yoga Journal*. She unfolded it and read it for the umpteenth time. It was studded with lush tropical photographs.

Here goes, thought Catherine. She dialed the number, and a female voice answered in Indonesian. Catherine was taken aback. She had not taken the language barrier into account.

"Oh, dear, do you speak English?"

The voice responded in a flurry of unintelligible syllables before a man came on the phone with an Australian accent.

"McFarland here. Brandon McFarland. May I be of help?"

"Yes, thank you. My name is Cath—" Her voice broke off. She had made the decision to start her new life under a brand new name. She took a deep breath and began again. "My name is Elizabeth, Elizabeth Donovan. I saw from your article in *Yoga Journal* that you take visitors at your retreat. I would like to come and stay for a while."

Brandon launched into his sales pitch. "Well, Miss Donovan, Bali is the Garden of Eden, a romantic island of remarkable serenity. There is much to see and much to do. Here at the Namaste Yoga Retreat, students of yoga find—"

Catherine cut him off. "Look … my child was killed in an accident."

"Oh—" Brandon paused before he spoke again, and this time, his tone was soothing. "How terribly sad. I am so very sorry! In what way may I be of help?"

"It's hard for me to answer that."

"I see. Well, Bali is a place where the heart can heal. Come stay with us. You will be in good hands."

"Thank you."

"Will you be coming from America?"

"Yes, from outside Chicago."

"Have you made flight reservations?"

"Not yet, but I will in a week or two. I have certain things to clear up first."

"Well, book yourself into Denpasar. Several airlines run indirect flights out of LA and San Francisco. My American students say

Korean Air is cheapest, while Cathay Pacific or Singapore Airlines are a bit more upscale."

"I'll go for the cheapest."

"Fine. Let me know your arrival date, flight, and time, and I'll send a driver to pick you up at the Denpasar airport."

Catherine's voiced dropped to a whisper. "Thank you." There was a click, and the phones disconnected.

Two weeks later, an exhausted Catherine arrived at the airport in Bali. Her fight began in Lancaster and had come down in Chicago, Los Angeles, Seoul, and ultimately Denpasar. She had spent nine hours sitting in airports and twenty-seven hours up in the air. The food she'd been served had not been appealing, and she had lost her Bali travel book at LAX. Furthermore, on the last leg of the journey, she had been miserably trapped in a seat that refused to recline.

Catherine finally hit customs in Denpasar, and the experience was quite unnerving. The customs agent spoke English of sorts, but with such a pronounced accent that Catherine had not fully understood his questions. She answered as best she could, but whatever she said had distressed him enormously. *Oh, God, they must think I'm a drug smuggler.* She was taken into a separate office where three uniformed men scowled fiercely at her before a bilingual agent intervened. She finally passed through customs feeling bone tired, utterly alone, and no longer sure that escaping to Bali was such a red-hot idea.

Without thinking, Catherine walked right past the man holding up a sign reading, "Welcome Elizabeth." Bewildered, she stood in the crowded waiting room, waiting for someone to meet her as promised. When no one appeared, she took her rollaway luggage and moved out toward the hot, dusty road filled with noisy cars and mopeds. She was hungry and thirsty and completely exhausted. Maybe it was the heat or the crowd or the noise, but she also felt a little woozy.

Once she left the safety of the airport, Catherine was besieged by throngs of vendors. She made the mistake of purchasing a bottle of water with an American dollar bill. This display of real money caused vendors to press even harder on her, hawking their wares in shrill Indonesian, each trying to make a sale. Feeling exhausted and claustrophobic, Catherine was about to climb aboard a jitney to nowhere when she caught a glimpse of the man with the "Welcome Elizabeth" sign.

Dragging her misbehaving rollaway, she elbowed her way through the crowds, calling, "Hello! Over here! I'm Elizabeth. Elizabeth Donovan. "

"Please. My name is Wayan. I'm from the Namaste Yoga Retreat. Our car is right over there."

Catherine sighed in relief. "I'm so glad to find you."

"Welcome to Bali, Miss Donovan!"

Oh, dear, I'd better get used to my maiden name!

Catherine leaned back in the seat and took a drink from her bottle of water. She noticed the car was immaculately kept and the seats were covered with thick clear plastic. She felt safe now that Wayan had found her. He seemed like a nice young man.

"Trip take two hours, Miss 'Lizbeth. If want, you rest," announced Wayan as he started up the car.

Catherine nodded. "Thank you." She leaned back against the seat and looked out the window as they drove through the bustle of Denpasar and moved east along a narrow mountain road. She abandoned all thoughts of sleep as the extraordinary beauty of Bali unfolded before her. The car moved past terraced rice paddies, emerald green in color. She remembered reading in her tour book that these very same rice paddies had been meticulously maintained for centuries.

Here and there, a glossy water buffalo appeared, and sometimes a flock of ducks flew by. It was picture-postcard gorgeous. Catherine could only wish she wasn't feeling so exhausted.

A map of Bali had been pinned to the back of the driver's seat. Tracing the map with her finger, Catherine identified that the glittering blue-green waters on her right were the waters of the Lombok Strait, which connected the Java Sea to the Indian Ocean. To the left, Catherine repeatedly caught dramatic views of an ancient volcano.

They drove through villages filled with small, thatched-roof houses. Occasionally, Catherine would see a man crouched by a cage with a rooster inside, talking to it and massaging its feathers. She remembered Katie and her Chinese fortune bird and leaned forward to ask, "Do those men keep roosters as pets?"

He turned around and grinned: "Fighting cocks. Fighting cocks. Birds need plenty sun, plenty exercise. Oops—" Wayan turned back to look at the road and swerved, barely missing a moped with a pig roped on behind the driver.

Catherine made a face. *That's it. No more questions!*

Through the car window, Catherine could see Balinese women in traditional dress walking gracefully on the side of the road. They were wearing sarongs of faded batik, and they balanced baskets of papayas, bananas, or coconuts on their heads. Bougainvilleas, hibiscus, and frangipani flourished, and villages were sprinkled with color. *Oh, Katie, I wish you could see this!*

Catherine pulled the tattered article from *Yoga Journal* from her purse and read it again. She practically had it memorized! "Candi Dasa is home to the Namaste Yoga Retreat, an affordable haven founded by an Australian yoga instructor named Brandon McFarland. His specialty is power yoga, greatly favored by the young, the muscular, and the fit. Most students, however, are dilettantes."

That would be me, thought Catherine.

From three pages of photographs, she knew that the retreat would be a simple arrangement of thatched bamboo huts in a rural seaside setting. Meals would be made from vegetables grown on the premises and served on picnic tables down by the sea. *It all sounds so peaceful.*

Still, as they sped along the narrow asphalt road, waves of fatigue began to wash over her. *Damn it! Why am I so exhausted?* Catherine tried closing her eyes, but that only seemed to make her feel nauseated. *Oh, Lord, don't let me be carsick!*

They traveled for almost two hours before they arrived at the sleepy seaside village of Candi Dasa. Wayan pointed to a nearby hillside. "Up there. Temple name Candi Dasa. Very old. Now in big ruins."

"Uh—" muttered Catherine, trying to keep from throwing up.

Wayan seemed not to notice her discomfort. He pulled up to the front gate of the compound and cheerfully waved at a couple of Japanese students who were seated on steps in front of the office. A houseboy scurried out, bowing slightly. "Welcome, Miss 'Lizbeth." The houseboy removed Catherine's bags from the trunk of the car. "Follow me, please."

Catherine followed the boy down a path lined with coconut palms. They walked past a large roofed platform where a tall, muscular man with an Australian accent was leading a class in power yoga. The class was filled mostly with men, their bodies glistening with sweat. Their moves were both quick and athletic, resembling those made in martial arts. Their breaths were measured and audible, but as the instructor observed Catherine's passage, his nostrils flared and his breathing stopped. A German man noticed and grinned.

Catherine had been assigned to the cottage closest to the sea, and it was more of a walk than she had expected. The air seemed oppressively hot and humid, making her feel increasingly faint. She leaned for a moment against a tree and then sank to the ground, her face in her hands. The horrified houseboy sprang into action: "Merpati, come quick!"

A lovely young Indonesian girl came running. Together, she and the boy assisted Catherine to a thatched cottage filled with flowers and bowls of fruit. The one-room cottage had a high, pyramid-shaped ceiling, with wood carvings adorning its creamy white walls. Pulling aside a swath of mosquito netting, Merpati helped Catherine onto the large, canopied bed and turned on the ceiling fan. The houseboy ran out and returned minutes later bearing hot tea and bananas. Catherine pushed away the food. "No, no … I couldn't—"

She shoved the netting aside, crawled off the bed, and stumbled into the bathroom, where she began to retch.

"I go get Mr. Brandon," said the houseboy. He raced off in search of Brandon, but the Australian had left the yoga platform and was nowhere to be found.

Merpati helped Catherine get back into bed. She soaked a towel with water, wrung it out, and placed it on Catherine's brow. The breeze from the ceiling fan cooled the towel. *How delicious it feels to stretch out in bed*, thought Catherine.

She closed her eyes and fell into a deep sleep moments before Brandon appeared in the doorway. Merpati reached out to wake her, but Brandon shook his head. "Let her rest. She's been through a very difficult time." He lightly touched Catherine's cheek and frowned. "Bit of a fever. Two days on a plane can do that." He turned to Merpati. "Stay right here with Miss Donovan. Get her anything she needs. Do not leave her side!"

Merpati nodded in understanding.

CHAPTER 20

The Call of the Mermaid

I T WAS LATE IN THE afternoon. Dr. Nick Kontos sat in his office in Sarasota, unable to concentrate. The application folder laid spread out before him, but he just couldn't seem to get started. He sketched out a solitary game of tic-tac-toe on the back of a discarded envelope. Finally, he pulled a slim packet of photos out of the top desk drawer. The snapshots were of Catherine and Katie in happier days, and they both looked radiant and joyous.

One photo especially intrigued him—a close-up of Catherine, her head thrown back and her long hair flying. A single dramatic gold earring dangled against the darkness of her hair, and she was smiling. It was exactly the way he wanted to think of her. It was exactly the way she always should be.

Nick picked up the phone and called Lancaster, Ohio. He had called dozens of times before, and no one had ever answered. This time, however, he heard a recorded message: "This number is no longer in service. If you think you have reached this number in error—"

Dejected, Nick slowly set down the phone. *Damn it, Catherine. Where are you?*

He stared blankly out of the office door when Lexi walked by wearing a miniscule skirt and stilettos. Carrying an armload of files, she entered her office across the way. Through the two open doors, Nick watched as she slowly bent over and reached for the lowest file drawer. From where he was seated, he could see halfway to China!

Nick rolled his eyes and fiddled with the stapler. *Ah, dear Lexi and her come-hither bottom. Well, might as well take the bait. I haven't heard from her dad in a long, long time. It's time to confront the seductress and see what's going on.*

Pushing the photos back in the drawer, Nick sighed, got up and walked across the hall. "Well, Dr. Knight— would you like to get something to eat?"

Nick took Lexi's smile to be victorious. "Sure. Why not? I'll be finished in just a few minutes."

He nodded. "Meet me down at the fish tanks. Some injured loggerheads came in today. I want to see how they're doing."

"Fine. See you there."

The basement floor of Gulf Marine Lab was filled with enormous saltwater tanks, and Nick set about doing his daily rounds. First, he looked in at the five wounded loggerheads housed in the rehab center. One of those endangered sea turtles was in serious trouble, but the other four looked like they'd make it.

At the dolphin and whale hospital next door, he found an injured bottlenose dolphin holding its own. Nick had been part of the team that had brought that one in, and felt personally involved in its survival.

Across the hall, a conservation laboratory for seahorses had been newly created, thanks to a Selby Grant on which Nick had slaved for nearly a year. Here, for the first time, fragile seahorses would be raised in captivity. That same grant had paid for a ray-touch pool where classrooms of children assembled to stroke the velvety surface of a stingray, one with its barbs removed. That defanged stingray was a big hit with the kids.

Nick checked out the shark tanks where carnivorous fish swam relentlessly back and forth, studies in perpetual motion. Four years ago, he had instigated daily shark-training sessions at Gulf Marine, and now these were one of the lab's most popular programs. Indeed, their research on sharks had received sensational press all over the world, and Nick was the man who had made it all happen. Truth was, he had Lexi's dad to thank for underwriting the project.

On the far side of the shark tanks was a separate pool where enormous manatees paddled about. These whiskered sea cows devoured bushels of lettuce daily, much of it donated by local grocers. The slow-moving mammals were forever being slashed by speedboat propellers, and Nick had embarked on a mission to save them. Lexi's dad had been in on that one too, having paid for the pool that housed them.

If the truth be known, the basement floor of Gulf Marine had become a showcase for most of Nick's grandest achievements. *I'm so pleased to be part of all this,* he thought. *In five short years, we've turned this facility into a world-class lab. I've been damned lucky to have had Lexi's dad along for the ride.*

Having reached the end of his circuit, Nick's stomach started to growl. He'd skipped lunch and was ready to eat an octopus! He looked at the time on his cell phone: thirty minutes had passed, and still no Lexi. What was taking the diva so long? Increasingly exasperated, he stood with his back to the dolphin tank, fuming.

Suddenly he heard a rap on the glass behind him. Startled, he turned.

There was Lexi, *inside* the tank, wearing a glittering gold bikini and swimming with two dolphins named Haley and Moonshine.

Laughing, he gave her his undivided attention as she proceeded to do an elaborate underwater ballet, periodically taking gulps of air from a nearby air hose. She performed classic 1940's choreography worthy of Esther Williams and Busby Berkeley, an intricate routine best described as erotic and lovely. Watching her polished performance, Nick could only shake his head in amazement.

In a surprise finale, Lexi broke with tradition, threw off her suit, and swam stark naked, slowly doing backward "Ferris Wheels" underwater. Elegant and graceful, this woman had a beautiful body and the audacity to flaunt it.

Nick burst into applause.

So, too, did the janitor, who had entered to mop the floors.

Lexi took one look at the gaping janitor and shot up out of sight, swimsuit dangling from manicured fingers. The chunky man chortled, squeezed out his mop, and swiped at the floor with renewed vigor, whistling as he backed his way out of the swinging doors.

Moments later, Lexi appeared, fully dressed and toweling her wet blonde hair. Nick smiled broadly: "Brava! Brava!"

Lexi beamed. "So *that's* what it takes to get your attention."

"You, Dr. Knight, are full of surprises."

"Better believe it," said Lexi.

Nick held the door open for her as they went out into the late afternoon light. They walked along the docks and headed for a nearby restaurant. He looked admiringly at her and grinned. "You sure made that janitor's day!"

"I was trying to make yours!"

"Hey, anything's an improvement over that damned grant application."

"I would think so!" exclaimed Lexi, a slight frown clouding her face.

Nick seemed not to notice. "Where did you learn to do all that stuff?"

"I spent summers working as a mermaid at Weeki Watchee when I was an undergrad at Florida State. It kind of jived with marine biology. Besides, it made my stepmother furious, which was a definite perk."

"Ah, Weeki Watchee." Nick had traveled as a kid to see that enchanted Florida spring so named by the Seminole Indians. He and his family had spent hours there watching live mermaids who captivated tourists with their underwater antics. If the truth be told, those performances had inspired him to take scuba-diving lessons.

He raised his eyebrows. "Well, aren't you the clever little underwater rebel! Come on. Let's go drink to all the killer mermaids!"

Nick ushered her toward a rustic restaurant by the name of Turtles. It specialized in raw oysters and drinks topped with maraschino cherries and tiny paper umbrellas. Besides having a Tiki bar, the waterside restaurant had wooden tables out on the deck, and a laid-back, beach-bum atmosphere.

They were met by a waiter wearing sandals, shorts, and a turtle-green shirt. "Inside or out?" he queried.

"Out," said Nick. The waiter led them to a table on the deck and pulled out a chair for Lexi. "My name is George, and I'll be your server. What would you like to drink?"

"Absolut martini," said Lexi.

Nick concurred. "Make it two, with olives." The waiter nodded and headed back toward the bar.

"Tell me—what's up with your dad? I haven't heard from him for a while. He's a really important player here at Gulf Marine. We could never have done some of the things we've done without his financial support and involvement."

"Oh, Daddy's been busy. He's been engrossed with a couple of start-ups. He hasn't forgotten about Gulf, though. He's just waiting for your grants to come through so he can match them."

"Well, that's good to hear. I was starting to get worried. As great as the lab is, it needs to keep growing."

"Oh, you have nothing to worry about as long as you continue going after federal money. Daddy's a big believer in making the government pay. If you don't get those grants, though, he might be a wee bit disappointed."

"Don't want that to happen."

"Definitely not. Daddy's a Scorpio, and Scorpios are famous for being cruel and unforgiving."

"I'll make a note of that."

The waiter returned and set down the martinis. Lexi smiled as they tapped glasses. Nick took a sip. Like any good martini, it was sharp and dry and designed to get your mind off your troubles.

He studied Lexi. She was a striking woman with a swimmer's short hair and beautifully chiseled features. Why was he so leery of her? Too much money? Too used to having her own way? Too shallow? Or was it just that she wasn't Catherine?

He took another drink from his martini glass and pushed those disturbing questions out of his head. *Hell, for all I know Catherine is gone forever. Maybe she was just an unforgettable episode in my life. I feel I've become obsessed with a fantasy. If I had any sense, I'd give it all up.*

"Why so pensive, Nick?"

"Oh, I was thinking of you and your vast array of talents." *Liar, liar, pants on fire!*

"How nice of you to remember."

"I never forget a fabulous woman." *Lord, save me from this stupid banter!*

"I never forget a fabulous man." Lexi gave him a sideways glance. "Tell me—do you ever long for the good old days?"

Nick shrugged. "Oh, that was years ago. I was in grad school. Besides, you were married to husband number one, if I remember correctly."

"Unhappily. Very unhappily."

"We *all* were unhappy then, and drowning our sorrows in lust and liquor."

"Best damned way to drown sorrows. Speaking of which, you have certainly been grumpy-faced of late."

"Let's just say that things have not gone well in the romance department."

Lexi gazed ever-so-innocently around the docks. She took a delicate sip of her martini. "Perchance, could she be the lady of the fantastic earrings?"

Nick felt a wave of anger wash over him. "Goddamn it, Lexi. You've been nosing around in my desk!"

Lexi shrugged. "I was only hunting for the application folder. Wanted to see which changes you made. Some pictures showed up. Cute kid. Yours?"

"That's none of your damned business!"

"Sorry— Sorry—"

Nick was surprised at the rage he was feeling. Lexi had intruded on something very private and important to him. Daddy or no daddy, he had to put a stop to it before she invaded his life.

He stood and leaned toward her, both hands on the table. "Look, Alexandra. Stay out of my desk! There is nothing in there with your name on it."

Lexi reached up and pulled him back down into his seat. Her voice soothing. "I said I was sorry."

The waiter set another pair of martinis down on the table. "Happy hour, two for one," he announced and departed. Nick downed two slugs of the newest drink and stared off into the distance. He wished he was back in his office.

Lexi touched his arm. "Look, I overstepped my boundaries. Forgive me." Nick met her words with silence. She gave it another shot. "Listen, Nicky darling—nothing gets a person over a broken romance quicker than a trip to the hayloft."

"That is so superficial!"

Lexi shrugged. "It's an eternal truth."

"Look, the only eternal truth I know is this: Thou shalt not bed down thy office associates!" Nick downed the rest of his drink. *Oh, God, I sound just like my father.*

"What about mermaids?"

"Can't have sex with a mermaid."

"Ever try it?"

"Nope. Whiskers rate high on my list of turnoffs."

"Aw, that was a manatee. You definitely need a roll in the hay."

"Look, the only roll I need right now is a shrimp roll. Do you want one?"

"Sure, if that's the best you've got to offer."

As he motioned to the waiter, Lexi leaned over and said in a come-hither voice, "Tell me the truth, big boy. Exactly what happened to that lusty Nick of yesteryear?"

He devoured his remaining olive. "Let's just say that he graduated."

"Oh—" Lexi sunk back in her chair. "Now there's a pity."

CHAPTER 21

Paradise, Sort of

In Candi Dasa three days later, Merpati went about her morning chores. She quietly swept and mopped the bamboo floors of Catherine's cottage and heated water to make tea. Finally, she walked down to the Namaste office and removed a tray of ice from an old refrigerator. She dumped the contents of the tray into a large plastic bowl, put cloth dish towels in with the ice, and returned to the high-ceilinged cottage where Catherine was sleeping.

Carrying the bowl of ice and compresses, Merpati pushed aside the mosquito netting and sat at edge of bed, gently placing a cool cloth on Catherine's forehead. A figure appeared silhouetted in the open door. Brandon had just returned from a two-day trip to the far side of the island. "How is she?" he asked.

Merpati shook her head. "She takes no food. Just sleeps. Three days now." Catherine moved restlessly, unaware of the people around her.

Brandon put his hand on her forehead and scowled. *Damn! It's more serious than I thought. She's bloody scorchin'!* When he turned to

Merpati, he gave rapid instructions. "Go get the doctor. Tell him to come right away. I should have called him sooner. Here, give me the bowl. I'll handle that." The girl handed him the bowl of ice and scurried out to get help.

Brandon was worried. For all his experience, he had not had anything like this happen before on his watch. Highly concerned, he surprised himself by becoming nurturing. He sat on bed and wrung out a fresh compress. Then he brushed a lock of cropped hair gently to one side and placed the cool cloth on her forehead.

Taking her wrist in one hand, Brandon looked at his watch as he took her pulse. *Seems normal enough,* he thought. She stirred, and one of her feet appeared from beneath the covers. Brandon took the foot and began to massage her instep. Her eyes fluttered open. She looked startled to see a strange man sitting next to her.

Brandon introduced himself. "Hi, Elizabeth. I'm Brandon. A little reflexology never hurt anybody. Good for the chakras."

"Brandon—" she whispered.

Her eyes drifted closed as he continued to massage her foot. "I've sent for the doctor. He's the best we've got. Good man."

Her voice sounded puzzled. "Mmmmm. What day is this?"

"It's Tuesday, darlin'. You've had a long nap."

"Mmmmmm," she murmured and dozed off again.

After he took a bottle of lotion from the bedside table, Brandon continued kneading her instep, concentrating on its acupressure points. He could not take his eyes off her face. Her short dark hair framed perfect skin, and her eyelashes were extraordinarily long, even without mascara. *Ah, Miss Elizabeth Donovan, you're a pretty one. All we've got to do is get you well. Who knows where this journey will take us?*

At that moment, Merpati appeared in the doorway with Dr. Nguyen. Brandon gently tucked Catherine's foot beneath the covers, stood, and then addressed the doctor. "Thanks for coming." Turning, he introduced the doctor to his patient. "This is Elizabeth Donovan.

She arrived from America three days ago. At first, I thought she was just tired and depressed, but now she's running a fever."

The doctor looked curious. "Depressed?"

Brandon nodded. "She lost a child in an accident not long ago."

"I see," the doctor opened his case and took out a stethoscope. "Miss Donovan, are you able to sit up?"

Catherine murmured weakly, "I think so—" The two men helped Catherine sit up as Merpati arranged the pillows behind her.

As Dr. Nguyen began his examination, Brandon left the room and went out to the veranda. A young German named Hans walked by on the path with several friends, each carrying towels.

"Hey there, Brandon! We're off to the beach!"

"Good on you, mates! It's the perfect day for it!"

Hans frowned. "How's the new American lady doing? I heard she was under the weather."

"I give you my word she's going to be fine." Brandon was a big believer in the power of positive thinking.

"I look forward to meeting her," said Hans, grinning.

"Oh, I'll bet you do," replied Brandon.

Squinting his eyes, he watched the tall, handsome lad stride off toward the sea, blonde hair flowing. *That damned German is after my harem,* he thought and frowned. He ran his hands through his thicket of ebony hair. *Maybe I should grow it long again. Give 'em some competition.*

Brandon's thoughts were interrupted as Dr. Nguyen joined him on the veranda, having finished his examination. The physician took a pad from his case, scribbled out a prescription, and talked in the short sentences of a very busy man. "Miss Donovan's temperature is high. There is congestion in the lungs. I've seen several vicious cases of flu in the past two weeks. Tourists at the hotel. Not quite SARS, but wicked nonetheless. Perhaps she picked up something on the plane. We'll start her on antibiotics."

Dr. Nguyen ripped the prescription off of the pad and handed it to Brandon. "Give her liquids, fruit juice, soups—" The doctor pulled a small bottle out of his case and placed it carefully in Brandon's hands "And put a few drops of this in her tea twice a day. It's an old Balinese remedy."

"Probably works better than the other stuff."

"Probably does," Dr. Nguyen said and nodded. He snapped his case shut. "All right, Brandon, the rest is up to you. Do your magic." The doctor moved quickly down the stairs and departed.

Brandon called after the disappearing figure, "I'll do my best. Thanks, Doc." Then he went to find Merpati and handed her the prescription. "Here, get this filled and sign for it. Take the driver. I'm going to rustle up some soup." As Merpati left on her mission, Brandon went into action. *Not to worry, beautiful lady. Three days of my homemade Australian soup and you'll be miraculously resurrected.*

<hr />

Inside the cottage, Catherine was half asleep when she realized that she was not alone. When she opened her eyes, she saw the specter of Katie sitting quietly beside her on the bed, Mr. Sunshine perched upon her shoulder. The child was wrapped in a beautiful sarong and wearing a tall headdress made of golden sparkles.

Katie smiled serenely as she held her mother's hand. *I love you, Mommy,* she whispered. *Please don't worry. You're going to be just fine.*

CHAPTER 22

Soup, Glorious Soup!

BRANDON STOOD BY THE LADY's bed, holding a bowl of steaming soup. When he pulled back the mosquito netting, he found her, pale and wan, dressed in a nightgown of cotton and lace.

He smiled approvingly at her. "Aha! A Victorian virgin!" Catherine melted back into her pillow. "Hey," he protested, "don't be scared. It's your all-purpose-yogi soup man! Here, try this." He thrust a bowl of soup toward her—a creation he had made from scratch in the office kitchen. It was filled with duck, carrots, cabbage, and spinach, all grown in the garden at Namaste Yoga Retreat. Truth was that Brandon loved to cook.

Catherine tried feebly to push the bowl away, but he persisted. "Now, now, young lady. Duck soup is the secret to getting well. So it's soup, soup, and more soup!"

Catherine protested. "Oh, not again—"

He placed the bowl on the nightstand and pulled her up to a sitting position. "Yes, my dear, again and again. Health lurks just around the corner."

Catherine groaned. "How many days have I been in this damn bed?"

"A long time," admitted Brandon. "We've gone through two thousand buckets of soup. Here, take another sip."

Catherine turned her face away. "I can't!"

He remained relentless. "Doctor's orders!" He thrust an enormous spoon of steaming liquid in her direction. Reluctantly, Catherine tasted it. "Another," he urged as he fed her a second dose. "And one more for the road!"

Somehow, she downed the third spoonful. Brandon smiled. "There. You look perkier already! Can you stand up? Maybe I can take you out on the veranda to get some fresh air."

Catherine frowned. "I'm not too sure—"

"My arms of steel shall protect you, milady. Up you go."

As they moved across the silken bamboo floor and onto the veranda, Catherine asked, "Who were those singers I heard last night?"

"There's a school for orphans here in Candi Dasa. It's run by a wonderful lady from India. She teaches the children to sing in English and Sanskrit."

"Why Sanskrit? I didn't know anyone still spoke that."

"Ah, it's the primary language of Hinduism, a root language, rather like Latin and Greek are to English. The orphan's prayer meetings are special. Want to go sometime?"

"Someday when I'm better. That would be nice."

"Well, keep putting down that soup."

The earthenware tiles were warm from the afternoon sun. Catherine stood in silence, looking over the verdant scene, the incredible beauty of Bali spread like a fan before her.

Like most Balinese houses, Catherine's cottage had its back to the sea. Instead, it faced toward terraced hillsides where rice was abundantly growing. Here and there, the hills would dip down, allowing a glimpse of the legendary Mt. Agung. This ancient volcano was revered by the Balinese, who believed that evil forces lurked beneath the sea, while goodness and virtue came from the mountains.

Standing on the veranda, Catherine drank it all in. She leaned lightly against Brandon and stared at the opulent beauty of the fairy-tale island. Her mind drifted back to a time when she and Katie had selected an enormous tome from the library, a coffee-table book filled with stunning photographs of Bali. Together, the two had happily stretched out on the bed to study the pictures, turning pages with delicious slowness, tracing terraced rice fields with their fingers, and pretending they lived on that faraway island.

She remembered how Katie had sighed, snuggling up into the crook of her mother's arm. "Oh, Mommy, that is such a pretty, pretty place."

"Yes, Katie, it's lovely," Catherine had whispered a lifetime ago. She had closed the book, hugged her daughter, and kissed her on top of the head.

Katie had looked up and asked, "Will we go there someday, Mommy?"

"Of course we will," Catherine had promised. But there was to be no "someday" for her precious Katie. There would be only pictures in a book.

As she stood on the veranda looking out at the rice paddies, Catherine fought back tears. The scene was exactly as the two of them had imagined those many eons ago. In an almost inaudible voice, Catherine whispered the words once again. "Yes, Katie. It's lovely."

Brandon smiled. "And so, dear 'Lizbeth, are you."

CHAPTER 23

The Puzzle

IT WAS EARLY IN THE evening six days later. Nick's car moved down the winding road near the site of the fatal accident. Up until now, he had gone to great lengths to avoid that road. For him, it would always be a place of terrible trauma. Still, he could not continue driving miles out of his way. It was time to take the bull by the horns.

It went well at first. To his dismay, however, as he approached the curve, the headlights of an oncoming car triggered flashbacks of a night he would remember for the rest of his life.

Nick thought of Luke's car as it hurtled down the road.

He recalled a rush of fear as their two cars almost collided.

He remembered watching in horror as Luke's car left the road, rolling over and over and over.

And then there was Katie.

Nick could feel his heart racing. He pulled into the first driveway he could find, which served a deserted house with a faded "For Sale" sign. He sat there for several minutes, taking slow, deep breaths while trying to regain his composure. Looking down at his shaking hands, he thought, *So this is what PTSD feels like. No wonder I didn't want to come here.*

As he sat in the driveway, the pale figure of Katie appeared in the window of the deserted house. She stood silently gazing down at him, and her face had a worried expression.

Nick did not look up to see her, but at some cellular level, he could feel she was there.

The next morning, Nick sat alone at his kitchen table. The treasures he had rescued from Catherine's abandoned apartment were visible all around him. The drawing Katie had made in the coffee shop was prominently displayed on the kitchen wall, while spread out on the table were photographs printed up from the forgotten disk—photographs of Katie, Catherine, and a gray-striped cat named Tigger. A small wooden jewelry box containing the Katie necklace sat on the black granite counter, while Catherine's discarded copy of *Yoga Journal* lay open on the table.

He shook his head. *Nick, baby, you are beyond obsessed! It's the first time a woman's got to you like this. I have to admit, though, the circumstances were remarkably compelling.*

He pushed the photographs around on the table, creating several different arrangements until he found one that he liked. *Well, these are my clues, and they're all that I've got. How can I use them to take me to Catherine?*

Nick got up, poured himself a cup of coffee, and sat back down at the table. He picked up the yoga magazine and began to scrutinize it. The title of the feature article was "Restore Your Soul in Beautiful Bali." To his surprise, he found all those pages were missing. Someone has carefully cut them out with scissors. The rest of the magazine remained intact.

All right, Sherlock Holmes, why would Catherine want to remove these pages?

He scanned the magazine for the publisher's phone number,

picked up the phone, and dialed, thumbing through the rest of the magazine as he listened to the ringing of the phone.

Finally, someone answered. "This is *Yoga Journal*. My name is Rainbow. How may I be of help?"

"My name is Nick Kontos, and I'm looking for a back issue of your publication. It was June of last year, and the featured article was titled 'Restore Your Soul in Beautiful Bali.'"

"We may be out of that one."

"Well, check." Nick drummed his fingers on the table and waited.

Finally, Rainbow came back. "You're in luck! We have exactly one issue left."

"Excellent!" Nick gave her his credit card information.

He picked up a snapshot of Catherine and Katie and studied it closely. In the photo, they were wearing mother-daughter dresses in stripes of bright lime and pink.

He thought of his mother and little sister, Meredith, and how they liked to dress alike. His mother had been a costume designer for the community theatre, and she was a wizard on the sewing machine. From the moment Meredith was born, there had always been a closet full of matching mother-daughter outfits.

As a kid, Nick had been envious of the relationship between his mom and Meredith, but as his world expanded to sports and girls and academics, he got over it. Indeed, Meredith became as much of a treasure to him as she had become to their parents. And when she died … well, the loss had devastated them all.

There was something remarkable about the bond between a mother and daughter, something beautiful that set them apart from the rest of the world. Catherine must have had that same kind of bond with Katie.

Nick looked at the photograph and remembered Katie's words as she showed him her drawing at the coffee shop: *That's me. I'm the one in the ballerina suit. See, I'm wearing my gold necklace.*

Nick smiled as he studied the snapshot. *That's you, Katie. You're the one in the pink and green stripes. And that's your beautiful mother beside you.*

He set the snapshot back on the table. As he drank the rest of his coffee, he saw something strange out of the corner of his eye. For one brief moment, Katie's dress metamorphosed into the costume of a Balinese dancer.

Nick blinked. *That's odd—*

He rubbed his eyes and looked back at the photo. The apparition was gone, and Katie was once again shown wearing her brightly striped dress.

Frowning, Nick carried his cup to the sink. *I'll be damned. Is that a message from the great beyond, or am I badly in need of glasses?*

CHAPTER 24

Amazing Grace

IN SPITE OF BRANDON'S PERSISTENT efforts, Catherine's recuperation had been filled with setbacks. She had contracted some kind of echo virus that doggedly kept returning, accompanied by an extremely high fever. So many island tourists had come down with this debilitating virus that the US Department of Health had put travel to Indonesia on its cautionary list. Medications had run low in Candi Dasa, and Dr. Nuguyen carefully doled them out to only his sickest patients.

Brandon had become totally infatuated with his Victorian virgin, staying by her side for hours at a time, reading to her out loud, and making sure she received only the freshest of foods. Still, her return to health took place at a snail's pace, and she gained only a pound or two of the twelve she had lost. A smidge of color had slowly returned to her cheeks, and he heard her laugh for the very first time.

Finally, Dr. Nguyen pronounced her practically "good as new" and said she was free to walk the grounds of the Namaste Yoga Retreat. Tonight was the night that Brandon would keep his promise.

He was taking her to the orphanage run by the Indian lady to hear the children sing.

Catherine sat on the steps of her cottage, waiting. It was 4:45 in the morning. Stars were still bright in the sky, and the moon was a descending crescent. Waves lapped on the nearby shore while fat, multicolored geckos yodeled their strange two-tone cry.

It was almost 5:00 a.m. when she heard the sound of footsteps crunching on the path and Brandon appeared. "Elizabeth, is that you?"

"Yes," she whispered, "I'm ready."

"Sorry I'm late. The prayer meeting is just beginning." Brandon took her hand and guided her down the dark path toward the same platform where he taught yoga.

Nearly twenty children from the orphanage were seated in a circle atop the platform, a mix of boys and girls. As Catherine and Brandon climbed up the wooden stairs, a flashlight flicked on, guiding them safely through the darkness. They slipped off their sandals and took seats at the edge of the circle, sitting cross-legged on pillows.

A small black puppy wandered onto the platform, stopped beside one of the singers, and licked his face. The child brushed the friendly intruder aside. "*Tuka, tuka, tuka!*" the boy scolded. The puppy looked soulful and then settled down at Catherine's feet.

An elegant Indian lady dressed in a green silk sari raised her arms, and the children came to attention. When she brought her arms down, the young people began a melodic chant. She conducted them from memory with subtle movements of her graceful hands, and the chorus followed her every direction.

The group performed intricate melodies unfamiliar to the Western ear in a language that was no longer spoken. Sanskrit filled the early morning air. The youthful singers had lovely, clear voices, and sang with the confidence of repetition. The group performed without instrumental accompaniment, and the sounds of sea and forest played counterpoint to their lovely song.

As the charcoal sky turned slowly to deepest gray, the chants and mantras morphed into song. The voices segued from ancient Sanskrit hymns to hymns of the Western world that were sung in English.

Suddenly, "Amazing Grace" rang out in two-part harmony, majestic in the predawn darkness. *How surprising to hear that here*, thought Catherine. She closed her eyes and listened to the profound yet simple song, recognizing in that moment that music was truly a universal language.

Unseen by the singers or audience members, a misty vision of Katie appeared in the nearby forest, leaning up against a banyan tree. Mr. Sunshine sat perched on her finger, warbling his tiny heart out. Amid the cacophony of tropical sounds, his little birdsong went unnoticed.

Catherine could almost feel her daughter's presence, and tears began to well up in her eyes. Brandon reached over and took her hand. "Elizabeth, I'm so glad that you're here."

Through her tears, Catherine's face took on the beginnings of a smile. *What a lovely man*, she thought. *What a kind, lovely man.*

The specter of Katie frowned and abruptly vanished.

CHAPTER 25

Lexi Rules the World

Nick glanced out his office window. It was another sultry summer day in Florida. The thermometer hovered around ninety-two degrees, which would hardly qualify as a scorcher in Texas. In Florida, however, this modestly high reading came complete with sky-high humidity. Visitors from more arid climates spent hours of vacation time downing sweet iced tea and piña coladas, muttering about how miserable they were, and vowing never again to visit Florida in the summer.

Air-conditioning was what saved the tropics. Like most other year-round Floridians, Nick felt reluctant to leave the coolness of the buildings at this time of year, and this particular afternoon was no exception. He sat at his desk at the lab, pen in hand, and faced an empty page as he tried to get started on yet another grant proposal.

Nick would scribble a few words on paper, look out the window, and then write a few more sentences. After an entire afternoon of jotting down words and scratching them out, he ripped off all the pages, crumpled them into a ball, and tossed it basketball-style into the most distant wastebasket available. The ball bounced off the rim and landed on the floor. Nick walked over, picked up the crinkled wad, and dropped it into the metal basket, where it landed with a papery *thunk*.

It was after five. The day had seemed boring and wasted. Nick sat back down at his desk, opened the center drawer, and pulled out a folder containing a handful of snapshots. He pulled out one photo and studied it. It was his favorite, a tight shot of Catherine, head thrown back in laughter, her signature gold earrings glinting against her long dark hair. "Oh, Catherine, where are you?" Nick muttered under his breath.

Lost in thought, Nick sat staring at the picture. The door swung open, effectively destroying his reverie. Lexi burst into his office, wearing a stunning ensemble in brilliant yellow and brandishing a bottle of *Moet & Chandon* and two fluted glasses. Surprised, Nick quickly shoved photo and folder back into the drawer before he got to his feet to greet her. "Lexi, I thought you were in New York."

"I was … for weeks. But now I'm here, and tomorrow, I'm gone." Lexi presented him with the champagne. "So open it."

"Okay. What are we celebrating?"

"The publication of my new book, *The Barren Seas,* appearing in bookstores all over the planet. It's on Kindle. It's on Nook, and it's being reviewed in the *New York Times*. I've even taped an interview with Charlie Rose."

Nick was impressed. "Wow! Out already? Some publisher you got there!"

"They believe it to be an extremely important book. Besides, Daddy owns the company."

"Ah, Good old-fashioned nepotism. I'll drink to that!" Nick wrestled with the cork, extracted it, and drenched them both with spray. With a flourish, he poured the bubbly into the two crystal flutes and clinked glasses. "To Dr. Alexandra Knight and her great success as author, mermaid, and hot-lookin' lady"

"Ooooooh! I like the hot part! Drink up! I'm ravenous, and I've only got a few hours before my plane leaves."

"Where are you headed this time?"

"Book tour, darling. I hit the international lecture circuit tomorrow."

"That's our girl."

As if she was practicing for upcoming lectures, Lexi paced the room like a golden leopard, gesturing dramatically. "I am here to inform the world that we have overfished our seas and polluted our waters. Creatures are born every day with three eyes and seven fins and forty-six tentacles. Life beneath the sea is being erased!" She paused, poured them each another glass of *Moet & Chandon*, and continued, "Before you know it, I'll be incredibly rich and famous just like Daddy! I'll get writer's cramp from signing trillions of books, and I'll single-handedly save the dolphins of the world!"

Draining her glass, she turned to Nick and gave him a predatory smile. "So if we're going to have sex, let's do it tonight 'cause next week, I'll be too busy."

Nick coughed. "Great speech … up to the sex part. I was thinking more of taking you out to celebrate with a lobster dinner."

"Lobster? Ethical crisis. Well, okay. The lobster I eat tonight will be my final forkful of seafood. Besides, I'm starving."

As Lexi set her empty glass down on Nick's desk, she caught a glimpse of the dramatic photograph face up in the open drawer, and her smile faded. Nick frowned, reached over, and firmly shut the drawer. Lexi's eyes narrowed. "Don't tell me you're still mooning over lady long-gone?"

Nick took her firmly by the arm and ushered her toward the door. "Come on now. None of that. Let's hit the Lobster Shack. Want to take separate cars?"

"Separate cars. Separate beds. Whatever." Lexi's stilettos made angry little clicks as she was escorted toward the door. Halfway there, she stopped. "Are you sure you don't want to ride in my Bentley?"

"Next time."

Their cars were parked adjacent to each other in the parking lot, and the navy Bentley was first to depart. As she slowly backed out, Lexi stared at Nick through the side window, her striking face framed in hot yellow silk, her eyes smoldering.

Nick remembered that look. He'd seen it many years ago when they had been an item. *Damn, that Lexi is one persistent woman*, he thought as he started the engine of his Pontiac Grand Prix. *She has everything in the world. Why in blazes does she want me back in her life? I'd just be one more notch in her diamond-studded belt.*

As Nick followed the elegant Bentley down the waterfront road, he allowed the slight haze of *Moet & Chandon* to dim his obsession with Catherine.

Face it, old buddy, the lady has vanished. There are seven billion people living on this planet. Who knows if I'll ever find her? Sure, she's the one. I just get this feeling. But maybe we don't meet up again until we're ninety. For all I know, we're doomed to be one of those amazing romances rekindled in a nursing home. Hell, by then, Catherine might not even know who I am. Time to put my energy somewhere else, some place where I know I am welcome. Time to concentrate on work at the lab.

The taillight of the Bentley flashed a deep glowing red as Dr. Alexandra Knight pulled into a parking place. As he prowled the lot for his own empty space, Nick's thoughts returned to the times in graduate school when he and Lexi had been together. It hadn't been bad—pretty adventurous, actually. Lexi was always a woman who knew what she wanted and went for it. Trouble was she wanted everything in sight. So why in blazes was she zeroing in on him again after all these years?

Oh, my God, am I about to become a gigolo?

CHAPTER 26

On the Good Ship Lollipop

IT WAS LATER THAT NIGHT and well after dark. Over drinks and dinner, Lexi had told of her adventures in Greece, her book, and her dreams, while Nick mainly sat back and listened. He could not help but be intrigued, for she was a lady with spectacular ambition. *Maybe we can just be friends*, he told himself over and over. *Good friends and colleagues.*

He held true to that belief right through the last dram of Kahlua.

Nick asked for the check and signed it. "We've had a lot to drink, Lexi. I think we ought to take cabs. Pick up the cars tomorrow."

"I hate to leave the Bentley all night in a parking lot. What if somebody keyed it? Let's walk for a while."

She had a point. "Okay, we'll go down by the docks." Lexi hooked her arm into his, and off they went, arm in arm, busying themselves with small talk. He looked up at the moon. It was a silver crescent against the blue-black sky, while the waters of Sarasota Bay lapped darkly at the white hulls of yachts moored near the restaurant. In her skyscraper heels, Lexi stood almost as tall as Nick. Now she slipped them off, for they kept catching between wooden planks.

He had forgotten she was so tiny.

"The meal was fabulous, Nick. I may not be able to do it."

"Do what?"

"Give up lobster."

"Well, you could cut back to one or two a year."

"Cut back? I'm not good at that. I'm a woman of excesses. I'm used to having all I want of the very best."

"Papa taught you that, didn't he?"

"My first solid food was caviar, and I ate from a diamond spoon."

"And you turned out to be a smart lady—brilliant, really."

"Medium brilliant. Whenever some professor threatened me with a B, Daddy gave the college a new building. Amazing how many A's I got."

"Going to college costs a fortune today. Yours just cost a little more."

"It was my way of giving back to my alma mater."

Nick rolled his eyes. "Rah, rah, sis boom bah."

"Actually, I'm quite capable. Just a little lazy."

"Anybody who writes a book can't be too lazy."

"I had lots of help." Lexi held her finger to her lips. "Shhh—"

Nick felt a pang of resentment. *I've been working on a book of my own for a three long years and had to do all my own research. Things are easy for people with fat checkbooks. There's something off about that.*

Lexi frowned. "Why the long face? All those ivory-tower PhDs have research assistants. I just hired mine."

"I know. I know. You rich folk live in a different world."

They had come almost to the end of the dock when Lexi stopped in front of a graceful forty-five-foot sloop. The hot yellow silk she was wearing was so brilliant it seemed to glow in the darkness. Turning to Nick, she said, "Enough about me. Let's talk about you. Are you still mooning over that lady with the Ubangi earrings, the one who lives in your middle desk drawer?"

"Possibly—"

"Do you remember what it used to be like with us?"

"Of course I do, but that was years ago. The fires of youth were burning bright."

"Well, I've never forgotten. I always thought I should have ended up with you. "

Nick looked stunned. "You're kidding."

Lexi shrugged. "Well, it took a couple of bad apples in my life before I could figure that out. But when the chips were down, you were the man I never forgot."

"Lexi, I'm not in the same place now. I'm looking for something different."

"Oh, I think you would be if we ever got it on. I'm a big believer in keeping the fires burning. It's the secret to eternal youth."

Nick frowned. "Honey, listen … this is a big step. Things have changed."

"Maybe … maybe not. Pay attention to the doctor. What you need is an intense sexual encounter to forever erase the memory of lady long-gone."

"Doctorates in marine biology do not count."

"Oh, yes, they do! They may be fishy, but they count!" Lexi grabbed the sleeve of Nick's jacket and pulled him up the gangplank and onto the faded teak deck of the forty-five-foot sloop.

"Whoa! Where are we going?"

"It's okay. It's my brother's yacht."

Nick was incredulous. "Your brother? No kidding. You *are* full of surprises."

"I go out in this boat all the time."

"Got the keys?"

"Forgot to bring them. It's all right. We'll just stay in port." Lexi gave Nick a tiny shove, pushing him down onto a cushioned seat.

"I take it you want me to abandon my principles," said Nick, not sure he had any left.

Lexi pulled off his jacket, one sleeve at a time. "Off with your principles, darling! Listen to Momma. Let me hear your pounding heart!"

Nick managed a feeble protest. "Think of the future. We've got to sit through thousands of meetings together. Is this really a good idea?"

"It's a red-hot scorching idea! This assignation has no meaning whatsoever except to bring joy to the participants."

"Hedonist."

Lexi grabbed Nick's shoulders and stared straight into his eyes. "Actually, the purpose of this coupling is to erase the memory of a broad who has unjustly abandoned you and vanished into the mists of time. You're the one I want, and she is getting in my way."

"Really?" In spite of himself, Nick began to respond.

"I have a deep, powerful need to reconnect with you. Of all my many lovers, you were the best!" Lexi climbed astride her increasingly enthusiastic associate.

Nick surrendered to the moment. "Ah, Lexi, you've been reading the *Kama Sutra*."

She kissed him passionately. They tore at each other's clothes and were half naked when a beam of light flicked on. A man stood on the deck, brandishing a flashlight, glaring at them in disbelief. "What the hell is going on? Get off my boat!"

Embarrassed, Nick scrambled to pull up his clothes. He whispered to Lexi, "Is that really your brother?"

"We were separated at birth."

"Damn ... we're in trouble."

The boat owner grew increasingly angry. "For Christ's sake, I should have you arrested! What kind of trash are you anyway?"

Nick zipped up his zipper and tucked in his shirt. "Hey, look. We got on the wrong boat. I'm sorry!"

"You come back here again, I'm gonna shoot you!"

"No, sir. It will not happen again. I apologize."

The boat owner shined the light in Nick's face. "This boat ain't called the *Nookie-Nookie*."

"No, sir."

"And it ain't called the *Fucky-Fucky* either!"

"Definitely not."

The boat owner kept his flashlight trained on them as they stumbled off the dock and headed back toward their cars. Once out of range of the angry flashlight, both dissolved into waves of mortified laughter.

"We could have been killed," gasped Nick. "Why did you say you had a brother?"

Lexi shrugged. "I thought you knew. I'm an only child. Come on. Let's go on over to my place."

"Hey, no way! I've come to my senses."

She appeared crestfallen. She put her hand on his arm and gazed in his eyes. "Nicky, you know I could change all that."

"No doubt you could, but the moment is over."

"Well, thanks a lot." Her voice turned sullen. "You just put a great big damper on my little good-bye party."

"How can I say this? We were never meant to be. Not now, not all those many years ago. You're beautiful. You're brilliant. You're sexy, and you are way too much for a guy like me!" Nick gave her a kiss on the top of her head.

She did not answer. Tears welled up in her eyes.

"Oh, come on, Lexi. You're leaving on a great trip tomorrow. You're going to dive all over the world, give lectures, save whales—do all those things you trained to do."

"I feel like I'm out there all alone."

"Hell, we all do. Come on. I'll walk you to your car. Maybe someday when we're old and feeling frisky, we'll try for another X-rated evening."

"I can hardly wait."

He opened the door of her Bentley, and she slid behind the wheel. And that was when he made a *big* mistake. In an attempt to be conciliatory, Nick reached out and ruffled up her hair.

Lexi pulled back abruptly, pushing his hand away. "Cut it out!" she snapped, and slammed the car door.

Lexi stared at Nick as he crossed the moonlit parking lot. She had zero tolerance for rejection, and was now mulling the evening over in her mind. *What just happened here? I can't believe that Nick would turn me down. That's not like him. And why in blazes would he mess up my hair like that?*

She found that gesture to be extremely irritating. It was exactly what her cousin, Lenny, used to do to her when she was a kid. She had never liked that cousin, and he certainly did not care for her—or any other girl for that matter. Boys were his forte.

Her observant, analytical eyes turned on Nick as he got into his Grand Prix and drove away. *If he cares, he's going to look back,* she thought. But no, he did not.

She frowned. *Stir things up and then run away—that was Lenny's mean little trick.* She turned the key in the ignition, and the Bentley hunkered down and lurched into the road.

CHAPTER 27

The Reign of the Infant King

I T WAS EARLY MORNING IN Bali a week or so later when Catherine awoke and felt a wave of nausea wash over her. *Damned echo virus,* she mumbled. Dr. Nguyen had said that most of his other patients were experiencing the same thing. She threw off her covers, stumbled into the bathroom, and slammed the door behind her. As she wrestled with queasiness, Merpati came walking up the path, dressed in a long batik skirt and blouse of white lace, carrying an armload of pink frangipanis.

Merpati slipped off her rubber thongs and left them outside on the veranda. When she entered the cottage, she placed the flowers in an empty vase, fluffed up the pillows, and pulled the sheets up tight. As she went to get water for the flowers, she found the door to the bathroom closed, and heard soft sounds of moaning and retching on the other side.

Catherine's fit of nausea soon passed. She poured water from a large pitcher into the sink and splashed it on her face. After she pulled off her white nightgown, she draped herself awkwardly in a green and gold sarong. She had not yet mastered the art of wrapping this deceptively complicated garment, and it came out all lumpy and bumpy. *Well, I don't care,* thought Catherine. *No one will see me except Merpati, who will certainly show me how to fix it.*

Catherine opened the bathroom door and caught a glimpse of Merpati looking worried. "'Lizbeth, are you all right?"

"Oh, that damned flu! Just when I think I'm over it, I start throwing up again."

"Airplanes. They bring great sickness from faraway places. I do not like airplanes."

Catherine had to agree. "They're wonderful and awful, both at the same time."

"Do you wish to sleep?" asked Merpati as she smoothed the bed.

Catherine thought for a moment before she responded, "No. Actually, I think I'll go out."

Merpati looked puzzled. "But if you're sick?"

"Oh, I'm better now. Maybe I just need a bit of sun. The doctor says that with the fever gone, I'm not contagious anymore, so I guess it's time to go meet Iwayan. He's sure to cheer me up." Iwayan was a beautiful golden brown baby who was eight months old, with a sunny, playful disposition. His mother, Lastri, had often brought tea and fruit to Catherine when she had been confined to the cottage. Lastri had begged Catherine to come play with her child as soon as she was better. She had even drawn a little map so that the American lady could locate their cottage.

"Ah, Iwayan—he is such a happy little boy. He will make you happy too. Here, I fix your sarong." With experienced fingers, Merpati tugged and pulled and finger-pleated the cloth into submission. Soon, Catherine looked sleekly attired like all the other Balinese women.

Catherine laughed. "Someday I'll learn to wrap the darn thing."

"Someday you will." Merpati smiled as she tucked a few pink frangipanis into Catherine's short, glossy hair. "I am glad you are better."

Catherine walked up the path toward the platform where Brandon was just beginning a yoga class. Ten or twelve students were in the process of spreading out their yoga mats. One young American student named Jennifer came careening up the path behind Catherine. Jennifer had gone swimming at the beach and stayed far too long in the equatorial sun. Her cheeks were sunburned and freckled, and her long reddish hair was a scramble of saltwater curls. She had wrapped a Hawaiian pareo haphazardly around her waist.

"Whoops! Watch out, 'Lizbeth. I'm comin' through. Running late for yoga class!"

"Slow down," said Catherine, laughing. "You're supposed to be serene, remember?"

"Never was any good at that part!" Jennifer stumbled up the steps and hurled her mat out on the platform alongside the other students. Catherine waved at Brandon, who smiled to see her up and about.

Catherine proceeded up a path that was lined with coconut palms. She turned in at a small bamboo cottage propped up on short stilts. The simple thatched building was elevated just enough to keep out the monsoon rains and to give the family's fat spotted pig a shady place to sleep on a hot summer day.

Catherine walked around to the back, where she found Iwayan sitting in a blue plastic tub on the porch. The naked baby was decked out in a wondrous array of eighteen-karat gold bracelets, one around each wrist and one around each ankle. A glittering gold chain also circled his chubby neck. Days ago Brandon had told her about the Balinese custom of infants wearing jewelry. It seemed that in Bali, babies were given gold to wear when they were born in the belief that gold would ward off evil spirits.

Catherine had laughed then. "A lot of Western women would subscribe to that."

"I'll bet," Brandon had responded.

There sat Iwayan, bedecked in gold like an infant king, happily splashing water all over the place, drenching his young mother, Lastri, who squatted protectively beside him. She looked up at her

American visitor. "*Namaste*, 'Lizbeth! I see you are feeling stronger today."

"Oh, I'm definitely on the mend." She smiled at Iwayan, who giggled and flailed the water even harder with his tiny fists. His bracelets sparkled in the morning sun, causing rainbows to appear on tiny drops of water. "Hey, look at your little guy. He seems to be having a wonderful time."

"Bath time is good time for my firstborn son. Come up. Be with us!" Catherine kicked off her sandals and climbed three wooden steps to sit beside the blue plastic tub. Iwayan splashed extra hard, and water flew into Catherine's face.

"Whoa," said Catherine, laughing as she gently splashed the baby back. Iwayan flailed at the water with his tiny fists, squealing with joy. Catherine was thoroughly soaked, but she did not care. In the heat of the tropics, the water felt cool and welcome.

The young mother spoke softly to her son in Indonesian, distracting him with a small plastic toy. "I'm sorry, 'Lizbeth. He loves to play." Lastri handed Catherine a small towel.

"Me too," said Catherine, smiling broadly as she dried herself off.

Lastri lifted the boy out of the tub and wrapped him a large white towel. "Bath over. Time for Iwayan to sleep."

"Here, let me do that," Catherine reached for the child, and his mother gently lowered her son into Catherine's arms. The bejeweled baby sat happily on Catherine's lap, cooing as she gently dried his golden brown skin. With eyes as round as dark chocolates, Iwayan looked at her and smiled. Her heart just melted.

Lastri could not help but notice. "Baby like you very much."

"And I like baby very much … very much indeed."

As she cuddled the little one, Catherine turned her head to hide her tears from Iwayan and Lastri. Her innermost feelings were both painful and bittersweet. *Oh, Katie, my Katie, I miss you so much. We once played like this. Remember?*

CHAPTER 28

Connected By Satellite

IT WAS EARLY IN THE evening two weeks later when Nick entered his living room in Sarasota and picked up a stack of mail. He rifled through it—Florida Power and Light, Teco Gas, American Express, a catalog from Lands' End, and finally, the back copy he'd ordered from *Yoga Journal*. After he tossed the rest of the mail on the counter, he poured himself a glass of scotch. He pulled off his jacket, sat down in his favorite easy chair, opened the magazine wrapper, and turned to page eighty-eight. There it was, the article Catherine had cut from her personal copy, "Restore Your Soul in Beautiful Bali."

Nick skimmed through the piece. It was all about a rustic place called Namaste Yoga Retreat run by a group of Aussies. As he read it, he found a phone number and consulted his intricate diver's watch. Twelve, maybe fourteen hours difference. *Must be morning over there. Well, I'll give it a shot.* Nick picked up phone and pressed a dozen or so numbers, and a telephone rang in Brandon McFarland's office.

A woman answered, speaking in Indonesian. Then a man came

on, and his voice had a pronounced Australian accent. "Brandon McFarland here. How may I be of help?"

"This is Dr. Nicholas Kontos calling from Sarasota, Florida. I'm trying to locate an American lady by the name of Catherine Scanlon. I have reason to believe she may be a student at your yoga retreat."

"Hang on. Let me check my list of students currently in residence. We also have some new ones coming in." Nick heard the sounds of papers being shuffled around before Brandon came back on the line.

"Sorry, Dr. Kontos. There's not a single Catherine Scanlon in the bunch." I also checked our upcoming arrivals. No Catherines. No Scanlons."

Nick frowned. "Perhaps you've seen her. Maybe she's staying somewhere nearby."

"Anything's possible. A lot of Americans come here. What does she look like?"

"Caucasian, with spectacular long dark hair that falls to her waist. I would guess Catherine is in her late twenties or early thirties, tall, pale-skinned, and slender."

"Long dark hair? American? Sorry. I don't recall meeting anyone of that description. The only long-haired American I can come up with is a redhead named Jennifer. Freckles and all that."

Nick felt a wave of disappointment. It was a moment before he continued: "Oh, well. Perhaps I'll call again in a couple of weeks just in case she's shown up."

"Sure, mate. Happy to help. Hope you find her."

"Thank you."

"G'day."

There was a *click* followed by a dial tone. Nick slumped in his chair. *Damn. I felt sure this was going to work. It looks like just another dead end.*

He finished off the rest of his scotch. *Nick, my man, the woman's gone. You may never find her. Get over it.*

CHAPTER 29

The Land of the Tall People

IT WAS AFTER SIX IN the evening a month or so later when Lexi unexpectedly appeared in the doorway of Nick's office at Gulf Marine. She came upon a grumpy and unshaven Nick hunched over a glowing computer monitor. Enormous tangles of research papers were spread out all over his desk, and two wastebaskets were filled to overflowing.

Wearing a leopard print miniskirt, button-tugging blouse, and ever-present stilettos, she leaned up against the door to give her own husky-voiced rendition of the Samantha role in *Sex and the City*. "Well, did you miss me, big boy?"

"Oh, Lexi. Back already?" Nick looked annoyed at the interruption but managed a distracted hug—the kind where shoulders got involved but little else—and followed it up with a brotherly pat on the back.

Lexi felt like a baby who had just been burped. This was not exactly the welcome she had in mind. She grabbed Nick and hugged him fiercely. "Mmmmm. It is good to be back in the land of the tall people."

He took a step back. "I heard great things about your book tour."

Lexi smiled and spread out her manicured hands. "These freshly lacquered fingers are worn to nubbins from signing books."

Nick nodded. "And counting money, lots of money!"

"Bushels."

"In that case, you're taking *me* out to dinner after I get these last two pages knocked off."

Lexi stood with her hands on her hips. "Well, that depends on what you offer for dessert."

Nick sighed. "Ah, Lexi, you never change."

She spoke in a voice infused with exasperation. "May I interpret that as '*thank goodness* you never change?'"

He frowned. "Take it any way you want. Frankly, my dear, I don't give a damn."

Her smile evaporated. "That was rude."

"Scarlett O'Hara said the same thing. Look, Lexi, I'm sorry. I'm tired. I'm cranky, and I'm not into playing games. From here on out, I would like us to be just friends."

To make his point, he reached out and ruffled up her hair.

There it was again—the Lenny thing.

Lexi practically arched her back and hissed.

Lexi's antagonism for her cousin had been epic. They had fought like cats and cats. It came as no surprise to Lexi when Lenny turned out to be gay. Not just plain vanilla gay but *neon gay* with an in-your-face, ultra-flamboyant, look-at-me streak. At her debutante party, Lenny had leapt out of the coat closet wearing a skin-tight black leather Batman suit, stunning not only his family but a room filled with two hundred guests.

Lexi had just turned sixteen. Becoming a debutante was the most important moment of her young life. She would never forgive Lenny for upstaging her.

Her dad pretty much disowned Lenny on the spot. Nephew or

not, he didn't go for the gay thing. No indeed! Daddy surrounded himself with *real* men who drank scotch, watched football, kept mistresses, and played golf.

In Lexi's world, this hair-ruffling stuff was way out of line. Some strange ritual practiced by the fairy folk.

But Dr. Nicholas Kontos wasn't gay—

Or was he?

As Nick walked back to his desk, Lexi stared holes in his back. Nick had once been quite the randy super-stud. In the ivy-covered rooms of grad school, he had been her boy toy. At this moment in time, however, things had definitely changed. All that silliness about office romances being off limits would have never occurred to the daring dude of yesteryear. Of late, however, Nick could never *quite* manage to get it on with her. Close but no cigar, in the Monica Lewinsky sense of the word.

Was all that pointless foreplay, or was it part of an underlying plan?

As she stared at her one-time lover, Lexi's eyes narrowed into calculating slits. For years, she had provided Nick with a road to her father's bank accounts. It was not smart of him to bite the hand that delivered his checks.

Years of analytic training came to the fore. In Lexi's mind, all human behavior boiled down to sex.

Could the photos of lady long-gone simply be some kind of cover?

Perhaps an unfortunate shift in sexual orientation was the *real* reason Nick had become immune to her considerable charms. It certainly would explain his extraordinary change in behavior.

Ever the scientist, Lexi made a calculated decision. She intended to explore this theory and observe.

Whatever she found, she definitely intended to share it with Daddy.

And it'd better be good!

CHAPTER 30

The Kecak Dance

Perched on his poison-green motorbike, Catherine and Brandon swooped over the curving roads of Candi Dasa. Women stood at the side of the road, baskets balanced on their heads and children clinging to their sides. An occasional dog came out to bark at the bike's noisy passage.

Catherine was enchanted. Papaya, breadfruit, and banana trees abounded, as did coconut palms and banyans. Steeply pitched hills lined the road, and the valleys between those hills were filled with terraced rice fields laid out in graceful crescents. She couldn't help thinking: *Oh, Katie … it's even more beautiful than the pictures in your book.*

Catherine saw enormous black pigs with pale pink bellies reclining near thatched bamboo houses. They seemed to be living the life of respected household pets, but she knew they were doomed to be roasted at some future feast. It wasn't a fact she wanted to think about.

"Whoa," said Brandon. The motorbike skidded to a halt, allowing a duck herder to coax his raucous flock across the road. Brandon turned toward Catherine, who sat balanced behind him. "See those birds? Each village keeps its own flock of ducks for the express purpose of aerating the rice fields. They play an important part in the process of growing rice."

"How's that?"

"When Balinese ducks hunt for supper, they shake their bills through the mud. That back-and-forth action aerates the soil. The crop grows lush and green, and the ducks grow fat and sassy. It's a win-win situation. "

"I didn't know ducks ate rice."

"They don't. That's not what they're after. They're searching for seeds, plants, snails, insects, and even small rodents like mice. Anyway, the food they dig up must be the right stuff. Balinese duck is prized as a delicacy. It's served in restaurants all over the island."

Catherine shuddered. "I've never eaten a duck that ate mice."

"You will," grinned Brandon.

As the last quacking bird waddled past, the motorbike pulled back out into the curving road. Catherine clung to Brandon's waist, delighted to finally be out and about.

A mile or so later, he pulled into an unpaved parking lot that served as the entrance to one of the larger Balinese Hindu temples. Two empty tourist buses were parked in the shade outside, having disgorged their passengers. The visitors were disappearing into the temple, toting cameras and sunscreen and chattering in a variety of languages.

Brandon waited for Catherine to dismount before he set the kickstand and locked the bike. He ushered her towards the entrance, for the show was about to begin. As they neared the gate, a sign loomed before them, one that appeared in front of hundreds of temples all over Bali. The sign was written in both English and Indonesian, and the words were startling to most Western eyes: "WOMEN IN MENSTRUATION ARE FORBIDDEN TO ENTER."

Catherine stared at the sign, hypnotized.

Brandon noticed the startled look on her face. "Ah, a bit of local color. Those signs are in front of all the temples. Some religious thing. Would you rather not go in?"

"No, no, I'm legal—"

"Then come on. Let's join the tourists." As he entered the temple, the sounds of the Gamelan Orchestra almost drowned out his words.

Catherine held back, frowning, transfixed by the sign.

A young Balinese girl who looked six or seven years of age scooted through the gate, her mother in close attendance. The child was undoubtedly one of the performers, for she was dramatically made up and encased in a tube of brightly colored silk.

Triggered by the sight of the little dancer, Catherine's heart began to pound inside her chest. Her breath quickened, and her head began to spin. She staggered to the safety of a small stone bench.

A cascade of images exploded in her mind, forgotten scenes from the night of the accident, traumatic episodes she had not yet dared to remember. Catherine fought to shut down these images, but her mind refused to stop. Relentlessly, her thoughts replayed the final night of Katie's life.

Catherine remembered wrapping the slender figure of her child in brightly colored cloth, never dreaming that within the hour, that fabric would serve as Katie's shroud.

She had rimmed her daughter's eyes with black and painted her lips with crimson. She had created an imaginary headdress from curled tentacles of silver foil.

"That's not gold," Katie had yelped.

Catherine had shrugged: "Silver, gold—what's the difference?" Katie had echoed her mother's words.

Now many weeks later, seated alone on a temple bench, Catherine's breath quickened. Memories pressed down upon her like stones, and she had trouble breathing. To protect herself, she had pushed away all thoughts of the night her daughter had left this world. Now tears welled up in her eyes as flashbacks of that night emerged.

These fractured memories were accompanied by strands of a sad but beautiful piano theme, heartbreaking and unforgettable. The music in her head conflicted with the piercing sounds emanating from the temple, but Catherine was too inwardly focused to notice. She sat like a statue, staring at the sign in front of the temple: "WOMEN IN MENSTRUATION ARE FORBIDDEN TO ENTER."

A look of puzzlement came over her face. *When was the last time?*

Brandon suddenly popped up in the entrance, clearly exasperated. "What's the matter, 'Lizbeth? Come on. There's a lot to see." Impatient, he ducked back through the gate and disappeared.

Catherine did not respond. She sat motionless in front of the entry, lost in fragments of a night she did not want to remember. Against her will, the tidal wave of images enveloped her again, and she felt drowned in violent memories.

Luke's features, twisted and deranged—

Smears of red lipstick across Katie's face—

Nails scratching the trunk of a muddy green car—

Catherine shivered and pushed the nightmares away. Her breath froze as she saw the little costumed dancer peek once again through the temple gate. *Oh, Lord! That child looks exactly like Katie.*

The sounds of xylophones began to swell as Brandon moved toward her. "The Kecak Dance is about to begin. It's really good! You don't want to miss it."

Catherine remained frozen, obsessed with an emerging question. *When was the last time? I've been so sad. I've been so ill. It just didn't seem to matter.*

Brandon studied her face. "Hey, are you all right?"

"It's … it's just the heat."

Mystified, he lifted her to her feet. He put his arm protectively around her shoulders, and then he led her across the courtyard toward four rows of benches where the other tourists were seated, vigorously cooling themselves with palm-leaf fans.

The overture ended, and the musicians paused, waiting for latecomers to take their seats.

Brandon motioned toward a large group of bronzed, shirtless men seated in a thick crescent several dancers deep. "Those are the Kecak dancers," he whispered. "They're the ones wearing red headbands and black-and-white sarongs."

The percussive sound of the xylophones started up once again, piercing the heat of the temple courtyard. The dancers' arms shot upward, and their bodies swayed in unison. They began to chant in voices that replicated the harsh cries of the monkey.

"*Kecha. Kecha. Kecha—*"

The men leaned first to the left and then to the right, hands raised toward the sky in synchronized motion. Their chant was relentless, its jackhammer sound powerful and compelling.

"*Kecha. Kecha. Kecha—*"

As the arm-dance unfurled before her eyes, Catherine's mind continued to reach deep into the unknown, unearthing forgotten memories.

"*Kecha. Kecha. Kecha—*"

The seated men swayed as if they were one. Catherine saw flashbacks of Luke's disappearing car.

"*Kecha. Kecha. Kecha—*"

A gong sounded, and the dancers splayed their outstretched hands. All Catherine heard were the sounds of a car crash and the heartbreaking wail of a siren.

"*Kecha. Kecha. Kecha—*"

Catherine relived the terror of finding Katie sprawled in a pool of crimson blood.

"*Kecha. Kecha. Kecha—*"

She felt the numbness of being questioned by the police and the kindness of a vaguely familiar stranger.

Tigger the cat at the open door—

The shattered photograph of Katie—

"*Kecha. Kecha. Kecha—*"

In a desperate attempt to escape the unspeakable, Catherine sought solace in the arms of the stranger. On the very night that her daughter had been killed, she had taken this man as her lover.

Katie was dead!

How dare he take advantage of her fragile situation? How could he have been so unfeeling?

Katie was dead!

How could she have been so foolish?

Katie was dead!

How could they have both been so stupid?

"*Kecha. Kecha. Kecha. Kecha. Kecha. Kecha. Kecha!*"

With hands outstretched, the dancers reached toward the sky, and the music abruptly halted.

Against a backdrop of utter silence, Catherine heard words she had said to Merpati that very morning. "What horrible flu! Just when I think I'm completely over it, I start throwing up all over again."

As Catherine's hands slid down to her belly, her heart was flooded with a single thought: *Could it be? Is it possible I'm pregnant?*

CHAPTER 31

The Australian Feather Ruffler

Nick stood in his living room in Sarasota, hammer in hand. He had just finished driving nails into the wall and hanging two newly framed pictures. The first was a print of the very same snapshot Catherine had carried with her to Bali. It showed a smiling Katie dressed in her flowered jeans and sky blue shirt, with Mr. Sunshine happily ensconced upon her shoulder.

The second snapshot had been enhanced, cropped, and greatly enlarged by the lab at Nick's request. It was the only picture he had of Catherine. Though not a professional shot, the result was a striking close-up, her head thrown back in laughter, her gold earrings showcased against long hair the color of dark chocolate. In this photograph, Catherine looked carefree and happy. It was the way that Nick wanted her to be.

He set down his hammer and studied these latest additions to his photo gallery, adjusting them each until they were parallel to the floor.

Nick had gone to the effort of having Katie's drawing matted and framed, and he now displayed it alongside her photograph. He never looked at that drawing without remembering his conversation with Katie that long-ago day in the coffee shop. Luke had indeed turned out to be the "bad daddy" the child had so eloquently described in her six-year-old fashion. It was almost as if Katie had known how their lives would turn out.

Other photos were hung on Nick's wall. There was one of his deceased little sister, Meredith, one of his parents at their forty-fifth wedding anniversary, and one of his golden retriever named Charlie, who now roamed the fields of paradise chasing cloud-tailed rabbits.

There was also a photo of Nick himself wearing a black scuba suit and holding an enormous lobster and another of him standing beside his prize-winning tarpon at *The World's Richest Tarpon Tournament* in Boca Grande, Florida. Nick's silver catch had weighed out at 220 pounds, with a length of eighty-six inches.

Nick had experienced mixed feelings over entering that tarpon tournament. He was, after all, in the business of *saving* fish. However, the prize money had proved too enticing. He aimed for winning the $50,000 first prize and buying himself a new four-wheel-drive Navigator that could tow a boat. Instead, he captured the $10,000 third prize, handed Uncle Sam his ransom, and bought himself a secondhand Jeep. *Better to capture half a dream than no dream at all*, as his grandmother used to say.

Nick squinted at his photo gallery and then shifted several pictures around so that his picture with the tarpon hung next to the portrait of Catherine. Satisfied with the arrangement, Nick glanced at his watch. It was time for another call. He made himself comfortable, picked up the phone, and dialed.

In faraway Bali, Brandon McFarland answered. "Namaste Yoga Retreat."

Nick took a stab at sounding upbeat. "Hello, McFarland. This is Nicholas Kontos. Sorry to bother you again. By any chance has Catherine Scanlon appeared?"

"No, sir, she hasn't."

Nick's voice deflated. He began grasping at straws. "Perhaps she's on her way but just hasn't arrived yet."

"Women do that sometime, mate."

Nick's groan was audible. "Well, I'll call again in a few days. I really need to find her, and you're the only clue I've got."

"Wish we could be of help."

Yeah, sure, Nick thought to himself. He could hear the wariness in Brandon's voice.

"Look, Dr. Kontos—there is no Catherine Scanlon in sight. Why don't you just leave a number in case she shows up?"

Nick frowned. *Now why do I think you'd lose it?* "No, I think it best if I called back, McFarland. Thanks for your help."

"Suit yourself," muttered Brandon, and the phone disconnected.

Nick scowled. *Damn. The guy must think I'm a stalker.* He plunked his phone down in the charger and moved toward the kitchen to rustle up something to eat.

As he walked past the photograph of Katie, he caught a glimpse of Mr. Sunshine out of the corner of his eye. The little bird's feathers now appeared to be standing on end in a display of ruffled anger. "Huh," said Nick, and he shook his head. Then he headed out to the kitchen and opened the refrigerator.

The snapshot of Katie came to life. She turned to lift the distressed bird from her shoulder, and cradled him lovingly in her hands, kissing the top of his small yellow head and calming him with whispers. Mr. Sunshine was soon happily chirping away, and his tousled feathers became smooth and glossy.

As he spread mustard on his sandwich, Nick heard a bird chirping. He paused, set down the knife, and looked around.

Did something get inside the house? he wondered.

Chapter 32

Which Path to Take?

CATHERINE STARED OUT AT THE blue-green waters of the Lombok Strait, which connected the Java Sea to the Indian Ocean. Over the past few days, she had spent hours walking this wide, deserted beach. She needed time alone with her troubled thoughts.

Could this be true? The stranger? The one-night stand? The encounter that never should have happened?

After she left the temple, she went straight to Dr. Nguyen, and he confirmed that she was pregnant. This revelation flooded Catherine's mind and heart with ambivalence. She had been given the gift of a new life, a child conceived in tragedy and fathered by an unknown man.

Would she be strong enough to raise this child by herself? Would she find the power to love another baby as she had loved her precious Katie?

Her head was spinning with unanswered questions. She would have the child, of course, but where would she go? What would she do? Bali was a strange new world, a place that had so captivated her daughter. But was it the land where this baby should be born? Catherine had money, but not much. She could stay for a while, but not long. She could keep the child or give it away, but she already knew she would keep it. Katie's life had been so short. She had left this world filled with promise. Perhaps this baby was being sent to finish Katie's dreams. Or was that too much to ask of an unborn child?

There was a saying she had read in the book on Bali: *The truth is one, the interpretations many.* Truth was that she was pregnant and she didn't even know the name of the father. *Conceived in tragedy*—how should one interpret that?

Catherine's head began to throb. What should she do? Which path should she take?

It was midnight. Catherine sat sleepless in her cottage, listening to the two-toned cry of a gecko. The snapshot of Katie was prominently displayed on the nightstand. She stared at the silver-framed photo for a long time, lost in thought. Finally, she kissed her fingertips and pressed them against the cool glass. "I think you're coming back to me, Pickle," she whispered. "Maybe you want to be born right here … in Bali."

Catherine drifted off to sleep. The snapshot of Katie went through metamorphosis. Mr. Sunshine trilled a tiny tune as Katie's flowered jeans and sky blue shirt transformed into the pink and gold costume of a Balinese dancer. A splendid golden headdress slowly materialized on the child's head, one that glittered and gleamed in the moonlight.

CHAPTER 33

The Revelation

IT WAS A GORGEOUS DAY at the Namaste Yoga Retreat, warm, bright, and awash with tropical breezes. Brandon and Catherine strolled toward the beach to join others for a vegetarian feast served in hand-carved wooden bowls. The five young men from Germany were busily heaping their bowls with curried lentil soup, mango-ginger salad, and fresh-baked whole-grain buttered bread. They flirted with red-haired Jennifer before they carried meals down to a picnic table shaded by palm trees and overlooking the sea.

A fresh group of adventurers were next to appear. They had all checked in at the retreat the previous evening. There were two girls from Hungary, a young man from Greece, another from Scotland, and a teacher from Sweden. All were excited to be in this exotic locale, ready to learn, experience, and explore. Jet lag, however, was totally demolishing their plans. By the end of lunch, all any of the new arrivals could manage was a long afternoon nap.

"No problem," said Brandon. He was secretly delighted to have Catherine all to himself. She was the most amazing lady he had ever known, beautiful and caring. He had important things to tell her, and today was the day.

Maybe.

Off they went on his poison-green motor motorbike, wearing T-shirts, swimsuits, and sarongs hitched up Gandhi-style into baggy shorts. The motorbike moved down the curving asphalt road, headed toward a remote swath of beach a few kilometers away.

The pale sands of the beach were warm, and the blue-green water of the Lombok Strait looked inviting. Palm trees swayed. Lava rocks glistened, and volcanoes towered. It was a setting right out of a Broadway production of *South Pacific*.

Brandon pulled the bike over to the side of the road and helped Catherine dismount. He smoothed down his disheveled hair. This was an important day, and he wanted to look his best.

Brandon knew he had a lot going for him. He'd captivated dozens of yoga ladies for many seasons, and he was justifiably proud of the lean, limber body he had worked so hard to obtain. Buff and handsome, he was aware that his build was a major asset. With that in mind, he pulled off his shirt and tightened his abs. Surely, the lovely American would notice.

Grabbing colorful beach towels from his overstuffed bike bag, Brandon spread them out on the thick golden sand. "Be seated, milady," he said with a flourish. Catherine's eyes widened as he retrieved a small machete from the motorbike, scurried up a sloping palm, whacked a coconut, and then scampered back down. "In yoga, we call that the Downward Falling Coconut," he said and grinned.

She laughed.

With a dramatic swipe of the machete, Brandon halved the coconut and ceremoniously handed her one of the pieces. He sat down to face her and made his toast. "Here's to 'Lizbeth, the most wonderful person who has ever entered my life." The coconuts "clinked" with a dull wooden thud.

His grand gesture was met with a look of apprehension. "Brandon—"

Emboldened, he leaned forward to pat her knee. "She was a bit sickly at first, but we worked that one out, didn't we, love?"

Catherine nodded. "You certainly deserve a gold star for taking care of a deathly ill woman."

"To the power of soup!" he declared, and they knocked husks once again. As Catherine sipped the fresh green coconut water, Brandon gathered courage and began his pitch. "Look, I know this sounds really corny, but in the outback when a man finds a woman like you, he wants to keep her."

She buried her face in her coconut.

Brandon persisted, heading right to the point. "I've been thinking a lot about you and me and us, where we are in our lives, and our Karmic connection. If the truth be known, you've run off with my heart." He paused nervously and began to ramble. "Besides, you've been through a bad situation. You're all by yourself. You're a long way from home, and—"

"Hell!" he muttered and jumped to his feet. "I'm no good at this!"

Hands on hips, he stared down at her and regained his composure. "Look, I'll say it clean and simple. I want you to be my wife."

Catherine choked slightly on the coconut water. "That might not be possible—"

Used to having his own way, Brandon felt a wave of irritation. He glared at her and frowned. "I thought there'd be more enthusiasm."

"You know so little about me."

"I know I'm head over heels in love with a silly Yank."

"My story is tangled."

Brandon sank back down. "So tell me. I'll listen."

Catherine set her coconut down on the sand. "You've taken wonderful care of me, maybe even saved my life, so I owe it to you to be honest." She reached out to touch his arm, a small gesture that sent electric currents ricocheting through his body.

"Go on—"

She sighed and looked away. After a moment, she began her

painful story, and the tale was quick and blunt. "My husband, Luke, was addicted to anything and everything. He lived to get high. His condition deteriorated, and he became violent. I took Katie and ran hundreds of miles away, never thinking he'd be able to find us. But somehow, he did." Her voice broke off. "Lord, I don't know how to say this—"

Tears began to pour down Catherine's cheeks. Brandon reached out to cover her hand and squeeze it firmly. In a voice that was barely a whisper, she continued, "Luke burst into our apartment and took Katie. He drove off like a maniac. A mile away, Luke met his death—" She struggled to get her breath. "He was killed in a wreck, and ... oh, God, he took Katie along with him."

Brandon's eyes widened. So that was the way it had happened! He was horrified. He longed to gather this beautiful woman up in his arms, but she pulled away. "Darling girl, you don't have to tell me anymore."

"Oh, yes, I do. This next part is crucial." She extracted her hand and inhaled deeply before she continued. "The night of the accident, there was a man who held my child in his arms as she was dying. That man was a stranger. He was the last person to see Katie alive. I was in shock. My thinking was twisted. Somehow, I felt this man was my link to her soul. Oh, Brandon, I don't know how to explain this—"

His eyes narrowed, and his voice turned cold. "You don't have to. I got it. You two ended up in the sack."

"Yes," she said softly as she looked straight at Brandon. "And he is the father of the child I now carry."

Brandon blinked. "Whoa there! You're preggers?"

Catherine nodded, and her eyes did not leave his face. He jumped to his feet and ran his hands through his thicket of hair. He looked away for a long time, and the silence was heavy. Finally, he turned to look back at her, and his voice was cool. "Do you love this man?"

Catherine shook her head slowly. "I think of him." Brandon frowned, and she reached out to touch his leg. "I am so very sorry."

"Does he know?"

Catherine shook her head. "No."

Arms folded, Brandon stared out at the horizon. Several minutes passed before he spoke, and when he did, his speech was measured. "You don't have to keep this child, you know. There are other answers—"

Catherine's voice was firm. "I'm keeping the baby."

Brandon frowned. "I'm in favor of kids, but I'd want the kids I raise to be mine. Besides, this bloke who fathered this embryo ... it doesn't sound like much of a relationship."

Her tone became steel. "I'm keeping the baby."

Brandon raised his voice sharply. "What do you know about this dude? What's his health? What's his background? Maybe the guy's a serial murderer or something."

Catherine's voice turned to ice. "I am *keeping* the baby!"

Brandon took a step backward. "Well," he announced, "I'm here, and your sperm donor is not." His voice softened. "Look, you need a man in your life, and I need a woman in mine." He sank down and positioned himself opposite her. "We'll find out where we are after your baby is born. Who knows? Maybe I'll even fall for the little bloke. We'll let some time pass. You'll see— We'll grow on each other."

He could barely hear Catherine's response. "I wish I believed you."

They stared at each other in total silence. The only sound was the sea lapping against the sandy shore, its pulsating tone enhanced by the cry of a seagull.

The specter of Katie appeared. She was dressed in the finery of a Balinese dancer, and she was scowling.

"That man's not my daddy!" she said to Mr. Sunshine. "He's *not* the daddy I chose!"

CHAPTER 34

Seeds of Doubt

IN A GLITZY APARTMENT AT the top of the Ritz Carlton in Sarasota, Lexi wrapped a thick white towel around her freshly washed hair. Swathed in a luxurious spa robe, she was talking to a friend on her cell phone.

"No, Dolores. There's nothing going on with Nick. I came all this way specifically to reconnect with him, and he just isn't buying. I'm thinking about moving on, maybe hooking up with Monterey Bay Aquarium. They've not only offered to promote my book, but they've asked me to head up their fund-raising."

"Is your dad involved out there too?"

"No, he isn't, not yet. But if I took over their fund-raising, he certainly would be. That's why they want me, of course. I'm the key to Daddy's checkbook. If I go, Gulf Marine will be left in the cold. My father's kind of a one-team guy. He'd never support both organizations."

"Well, what's stopping you?"

"Nick, of course. I never seem to get over him. Unlike other toads

I've known and loved, he's a quality prince. I thought that maybe if we worked side by side for a while, things would start sparking. I thought he'd be impressed with my book. I thought he'd be impressed with my dad's contributions. I thought he'd be impressed with my underwater swimming."

"You certainly didn't pull any punches!"

"Well, he sure hasn't been appreciative!" Annoyed, Lexi switched the phone to speaker and tossed it onto the bed. She went about unwrapping her hair while Dolores expressed commiseration. As she toweled her head with a vengeance, Lexi could hear only occasional burbles.

"I can't believe it either, Dolo. I even pulled the clothes off that man! Nick Kontos of all people—why would he turn into a soggy vegetable?"

Dolores's words came back in a tirade. "You think *you* have it bad? Well, let me tell you—" She angrily clucked out her own tale of erotic deceit and skullduggery.

With every salacious revelation, Lexi was horrified to find she was nodding in recognition. "You're kidding! Arnold? What a bummer. Is *that* why you broke up?"

Dolores's voice doubled in speed and in decibels. Lexi couldn't believe her ears. "And you didn't see *anything* strange going on?"

A stream of four-letter shrieks poured out of the speaker.

Lexi blinked. "Arnold … bisexual? Who would have guessed!"

As the tirade continued, Lexi groaned, "Those are *exactly* the characteristics I've been seeing in Nick. All those odd, distracted behaviors. The man is not one bit interested in hooking up with me. So what does that mean, Dolo? Do you think Nick's changed his sexual orientation?"

"Why not?" said Dolores. "It's all the rage. Bye, honey. Gotta run. But hey, don't forget about AIDS. Better get checked."

"Shit!" Lexi knocked the phone off the bed like a hockey puck. The conversation had left her feeling volcanically angry. She stared at herself in the mirror and watched her perfectly plucked eyebrows merge into a frown.

Does Dolores know something I don't know? If her crazy hypothesis checks out, I'm heading for Monterey with Daddy in tow. That would hit Nick in the moneybags, right where it hurts.

CHAPTER 35

Leaving Indonesia

BRANDON SAT IN HIS OFFICE, wrestling with paperwork. He wasn't too keen on that sort of thing, but hey, somebody had to do it. He had spent three tortuous hours in hand-to-hand combat with Namaste's bills and correspondence, and he was delighted to be interrupted.

He jumped to his feet as Catherine came through the door. "Hey, 'Lizbeth. Take me away from this damned computer. It's not my bowl of rice. I'm nothing but a Bushie."

Catherine frowned. "Beg pardon?"

"Oh, I'm not referring to your former presidents. It's Aussie-speak for 'country boy.' Sit down. Sit down." Brandon ushered her into a chair. "Glad you're here. There's something important we've got to discuss."

"Really? What's that?"

"Guess what, dear lady? It's time to for us go abroad!" He slapped one hand upon his knee.

A wary look came across Catherine's face. "Meaning?"

"Every foreign visitor is required to leave Indonesia for several days once every six months. It's the law. Take a look at your visa. It's written in fine print."

Catherine blinked. "You're kidding. That's a bit of a curve."

Brandon shrugged. "It happens to all us foreign blokes. I'm almost due for my exodus, and they certainly won't let you get on a plane when you're big as a house. So here's what I propose: fly with me to Australia and meet my folks. The outback's a great place. We'll only be gone for a fortnight, and then you'll be good to stay in Bali for another six months."

Catherine got up and walked to the window. She stared out at the forest of bamboo and banana trees and shook her head. "I don't know what to say—"

He chucked her cheerfully under the chin. "You really don't have a choice, love. You've got to get out of Indonesia."

"You're sure?"

"I am. It's time for us visitors to go walkabout."

"Oh, it seems so … inevitable."

"It is."

"Any other time I'd love to go." Her voice broke off, and she stared at him. "May I be honest? Can we do this trip and just be friends?"

He shrugged. "Sure, 'Lizbeth. Friends. Friends with benefits. We'll do whatever you want."

"There won't be any misunderstandings?"

"There won't be."

"Well then, I guess we're off to meet your folks."

"Beaut!" Brandon could barely contain his delight. "Wait 'til you meet my mom. She's going to love you!"

Chapter 36

Walkabout

Two weeks later, Catherine found herself gazing out the window of a Virgin Australia plane while Brandon pointed out the finer points of Sydney Harbor. On this sun-drenched morning, the harbor was painted a vibrant blue, dotted with hundreds of sailboats, cruise boats, and ferries.

Catherine leaned forward in her seat to take it all in.

Brandon took on the role of tour director. "See that little island right in the middle of the harbor, the one with the tower? That's Fort Denison. In the old days, it was a jail, but now it's used for weddings. Guess that's kind of the same thing, huh?" Brandon gave Catherine a little nudge, but she ignored him.

Undaunted, he continued, "Sydney was settled in 1788, nearly twenty years after Captain Cook landed. Now more than five million Aussies live here."

"It's beautiful!"

"Sure is! Look! There's the Rocks, the Circular Quay, and Taronga

Park Zoo. Up ahead's the Botanical Gardens and our famous Sydney Opera House. It was designed to look like the sails of a ship."

"The real thing looks impressive."

"Oh, and that's the Sydney Harbor Bridge. Opened in '32. Locals call it *The Coat Hanger* for obvious reasons. They actually let people climb it." Brandon looked back at Catherine and grinned. "Well, not when they're preggers, of course. Maybe next trip. Anyway, it takes up to three hours to scale it. You're harnessed to a line, and they make you wear a bridge suit. Pretty adventurous, huh?"

Catherine shook her head. "Too much for me."

"Hey, buckle your seat belt. We're about to land."

They were met at the Sydney Airport by Brandon's father, Kevin McFarland, a lean, gangly rancher in his sixties. To Catherine, he looked like the Marlborough Man. "Welcome to Brandon's world," said Mr. McFarland. "Hope you like life in the bush."

She had hoped for a bit of sightseeing first, but Mr. McFarland could not get out of Sydney fast enough. "Too much city for me!" he muttered. He hailed a cab and headed straight for the small nearby airport, where his 1998 Cessna 172-S Skyhawk sat waiting. Like most ranchers who lived in the outback, the plane was his primary means of transportation.

The Skyhawk was a workhorse designed to hold four passengers and hardly anything else. With baggage stacked on the narrow backseat, there was little room left for sitting.

"Maybe I could fit in back there," said Catherine, certain Brandon would insist that she ride up front. To her surprise, he cheerfully accepted. *Chivalry's dead in the outback,* she grumbled as she climbed over suitcases. *Guess that's how they do things Down Under.*

"Hand me that duffle," barked Mr. McFarland. "Gotta balance the plane." Catherine did as she was told, and Brandon set the duffle on the floor beneath his feet.

The plane shuddered and shook as its engine revved up, and then it bounced down the runway. Catherine tried for one last glimpse of Sydney Harbor, but a suitcase was in her way.

The cockpit filled with engine sounds as the Cessna circled and headed inland. "Pretty good tailwinds," shouted Mr. McFarland. "We'll be home in less than three hours." *Golly*, she thought. *Can I travel that far without having to pee? Fat chance that they'd stop at a restroom.*

Occasional bits of conversation would float toward the back of the plane. Catherine heard the words "rugby" and "bloody" a lot, and sometimes she even heard the word "cricket." She couldn't help thinking, *Brandon's certainly reverting to his roots. Looks like the nurturing yogi got left behind at Candi Dasa.*

The drone of the engine was making her sleepy. Leaning against a suitcase, she nodded off and began to dream.

My golden earrings glitter against my tangled hair. I carry a tray of glasses through a purple swinging door.

There stands Katie, using the palm of her hand to wipe a slash of green across a yellow wall. She is wearing a bright pink smock. She turns to show a visitor the mural she is painting.

The stranger studies the mural, and then he smiles. He is tall and handsome, and he wears a rucksack. I wonder who he is.

Katie turns toward me and speaks in a bell-like voice, "He'd make a very good daddy," she says.

Startled, Catherine's eyes flew open.

"Tighten your seat belts," yelled Mr. McFarland. "We're in for a bumpy ride."

CHAPTER 37

The Secret of a Great Pavlova

THE SUN WAS JUST SETTING when the Skyhawk came down on the landing strip at the McFarland sheep station, a few hundred miles from Adelaide. As the plane taxied toward the ranch house, Brandon saw his mother running out to meet them. She wore a bright red sweater and a denim dress, and Bosco, the dog, was trotting by her side.

The men deplaned first. Brandon turned to help 'Lizbeth, who was moving stiffly, probably from having slept in such odd positions. There were lots of hellos, hugs, greetings, and welcomes all around. Brandon knew in a moment that his mother was delighted to finally have visitors. "At last," cried Cynthia McFarland. "It gets pretty lonely out here with nobody to talk to except an occasional jumbuck or jackaroo."

Brandon handed the duffle down to 'Lizbeth and then pulled the rest of the luggage out of the back of the Skyhawk. "Hey, Dad, great landing! You usually bounce around like a wallaby."

Mr. McFarland went about putting his plane to bed. "Well, I had to impress your girlfriend! Everybody up for a beer?"

'Lizbeth shook her head. "Not for me, thanks."

Mrs. McFarland grabbed one side of the duffle. "Oh, but you must have a taste of our beer, love," she insisted. "We make it ourselves. A shandy perhaps?"

"Well … just a tiny taste—"

They entered the spacious, rustic ranch house. Everything was built out of rose colored wood, except for the fireplace, which was enormous and constructed from mottled river stone. Two guest bedrooms were tucked away in a huge upstairs loft, and each of these rooms had a double bed covered with a handmade quilt. "I sewed them myself," exclaimed Cynthia McFarland. "It was a big job. Took more than a year to finish them up."

The men hustled the suitcases up the stairs and set them down on waiting racks. Brandon put 'Lizbeth in the front bedroom, for that was the room with the view.

Cynthia McFarland announced matter-of-factly, "I don't know what sleeping arrangement you kids have. I've put you both upstairs so you can sort it out."

Brandon grinned. "Fine with me." His mother was used to his shenanigans.

Mrs. McFarland noticed 'Lizbeth blushing. "Don't be embarrassed, sweetie. This is a sheep station. Sex is no big deal around here!"

"That's enough, Mum—"

"Oh, I do talk too much, don't I?" his mother said and chuckled.

Truth was that Brandon had brought many girls home from Bali over the years. Most he had slept with, and a few had not. To Brandon's chagrin, his father had laughingly referred to these visits as "Brandon's semiannual sexodus." *Oh, God. I hope Dad doesn't say that to 'Lizbeth,* thought Brandon. He made a mental note to tell his father to cool it.

'Lizbeth stayed upstairs to unpack and shower while the others went back downstairs. Brandon whispered to his mum, "This one is very important to me. I don't know where it's going, but she's special. Please tell Dad not to embarrass me. I'd like this relationship to work."

Mrs. McFarland patted his arm. "Good on you, honey. It's about time you married, settled down, and gave me a couple of ankle-biters."

Brandon frowned. "It's not quite there yet, Mum. I'm taking it slow."

"That's a first," said his mother, laughing.

Brandon sighed. This situation was different. The last thing he wanted to do was to talk it over with his mum! For the moment, it was enough to have 'Lizbeth there in his childhood home. He was certain his family would love her. He wasn't so sure how she'd take to his folks.

Despite Brandon's vow of patience, a question kept nagging at the back of his mind: *I wonder when she'll invite me to share her bed.*

The house was soon filled with the fragrance of a freshly cooked meal. Mrs. McFarland had gathered armloads of vegetables from her garden that very morning. She had also made the meringue base for Brandon's favorite dessert, a pavlova topped with fresh whipped cream and slices of kiwi fruit. She prided herself on making the perfect meringue—brown and crunchy on the outside and slightly moist on the inside. Not every cook could pull that off, but Cynthia McFarland knew how to do it. Her grandmother had taught her the secret of making a great pavlova when she was only nine.

As Mrs. McFarland moved busily around the kitchen, an old orange cat stared lazily at her. "Well, Mango, what do you think?

Is 'Lizbeth the one? She'd be good, I think. But she'd need to learn how to make a mean pavlova."

Mango meowed his approval and hunkered down.

Two hours later, the three McFarlands and their guest were seated around the dinner table, staring at the remains of a sumptuous feast. Thoroughly sated, Brandon leaned back in his chair, his hand on his stomach: "Well, Mum, you did it again!"

"The lamb was fabulous!" 'Lizbeth chimed in.

Cynthia McFarland beamed. "We raised it ourselves. It's quite fresh. Dad butchered it for the occasion."

"Oh—" 'Lizbeth made a face.

Brandon laughed. "She thinks that meat is born at the supermarket, wrapped in cellophane."

"Ranch life surely wreaks havoc with your fantasies," said Mrs. McFarland, smiling. "Well now … how 'bout a cup of tea? Shall I put the kettle on?"

"Yes, please. I'd love some," 'Lizbeth jumped up. "Excuse me. I'm going to go get my sweater. Be right back."

Mrs. McFarland began to clear the table, but Brandon stopped her by jumping to his feet. "Sit down, Mum. I'll do it." He carried the plates off into the kitchen.

Mr. and Mrs. McFarland watched the lovely young woman as she climbed the stairs. In her thin summer dress, she looked busty and a bit curvy. "That girl has a glow about her," whispered Mrs. McFarland to her husband. "I wonder if she might be pregnant."

"That's m'boy! Us McFarlands are big on shotgun weddings!" He nudged his wife and gave her a wink.

Mrs. McFarland furrowed her brow. "Seriously, Kevin, it would be good for Brandon to get married."

"Sure would," he agreed, his voice gravelly. "Maybe then he'd come to his senses, move back, and give me a hand in the shearing shed."

Mrs. McFarland shrugged. "Well, it would certainly be better than teaching yoga in la-la land."

"More manly, I'd say. Much more manly."

Brandon stood at the sink, scraping dishes. He was thinking how well things were going between 'Lizbeth and his folks. He felt good about being in Australia. Who knows? He might even move back and take over the ranch someday.

It was nice having 'Lizbeth by his side. Maybe this thing about her being pregnant was tolerable. He didn't like it, of course, but it's not like the embryo's dad had ever been a real player in her life.

Still, what was he going to do with another man's child? The situation still troubled him. Maybe he could convince her to put the kid up for adoption—

It was two in the morning. Catherine lay sleeping beneath the quilt in the McFarland guest room. She tossed restlessly as she dreamed not of Brandon but rather of the unidentified stranger. Her mind was peppered with erotic flashbacks of their brief encounter, moments filled with passion but also with great kindness and concern. In this nocturnal fantasy, Catherine heard herself say, "It's better if I do not know your name."

"It's Nicholas. Nicholas Kon—"

In her dream, Catherine was suddenly jerked up against the ceiling. She flew round and round the room, cawing, "No names! No names!" As she leaned down, she clapped her hand over the stranger's mouth, and the dream abruptly ended.

Catherine's eyes flew open, and she sat bolt upright in bed. "Nicholas—" she whispered.

Catherine wrapped herself in the quilt and went to sit in a rocking chair by the window. Moonlight streamed in so brightly that she could barely see the Southern Cross. She rocked slowly back and forth, listening to her own inner thought.

Tell me, little unborn baby. What should I do? I only knew your father for a moment. I have no idea who he really is. I think about him sometimes now. We shared a remarkable night, one I will never forget because it has brought you into being. You're a part of him. And you're a part of me. Brandon might make you a very nice daddy. I'd bet that he'd learn to love you. Still, I find myself wondering about your father, a man by the name of Nicholas.

Catherine continued to rock back and forth as she gazed toward the constellations.

In the bedroom next door, Brandon awoke to the creaking sounds of the rocking chair. *Dollars to dingoes she's thinking of me,* he thought and grinned. He padded over to her door and tapped on it lightly. When he received no answer, he turned the handle found it locked.

The sounds of the rocking chair did not slow or stop.

Huh! First time that's ever happened.

Brandon made his way back to his room and crawled beneath the quilt. *Ah, rejection,* he sighed. *The world's most powerful aphrodisiac. That lady is out to capture my heart.*

CHAPTER 38

The Dog with the Mismatched Eyes

THE FORTNIGHT WAS ALMOST OVER. Catherine and Mrs. McFarland had become close friends. The older woman had shown the younger woman the secrets of making a great pavlova, while the younger woman had taught her the finer points of playing Scrabble. From Catherine's point of view, life in the outback seemed isolated and hard, but Mrs. McFarland appeared to relish it. She filled her hours with knitting and sewing or tending the garden and putting up jars of jam.

As their friendship blossomed, Catherine went so far as to share a treasured snapshot of Katie that she always kept in her wallet. However, this time when she pulled it out, there was a sharp crease across Katie's face that made her look sullen and angry. "I must have folded my wallet wrong or something," apologized Catherine. "Katie never looked like that. She was a beautiful, happy child. I must have that photo disk somewhere. I'll get a new print."

Mrs. McFarland patted her arm. "I'm sure Katie was a beauty, dear, just as you are." The two women smiled, and Catherine felt warm and welcome.

It was the day they were leaving for Bali. Brandon and Catherine leaned on the split-rail fence, watching Bosco patrol a disobedient flock of sheep. A few of the curly gray creatures had wandered off to graze in the shade of a eucalyptus tree, a situation that made the dog increasingly restless.

Bosco had worked the McFarland Sheep Ranch since he was a pup. An Australian shepherd, he was a blue merle with a patchwork coat of mottled black and gray. His eyes were of two different colors—one brown, one blue—which gave him a curious expression. Bosco was a dog with a mission, and he took his job very seriously. At Brandon's command, he scrambled off to bring back the wayward sheep, a goal he accomplished with a minimum number of nips and barks.

"Amazing," marveled Catherine.

"Oh, he's a great dog," exclaimed Brandon. He turned to smile at Catherine. "And you, my dear 'Lizbeth, are a great lady. My folks love you just as much as I do."

Catherine got a strange feeling in the pit of her stomach and turned away. "I like your parents too, Brandon. They are super people, but—"

A perplexed look came across Brandon's face. "What's wrong? I thought girls liked this sort of thing."

A wave of panic came over Catherine. "This is so difficult. I do care about you, Brandon."

Brandon frowned. "Go on—"

She took a deep breath before she dove in, unsure of how her words would end up sounding. "I don't want to lie to you. You and your family are very dear. But I've got to be truthful. I find myself thinking more and more about the father of my child."

Brandon's face clouded over. He stared at her, frowning. Then he shrugged: "Natural enough … under the circumstances. But hey, is this sperm donor thinking of you? Does he even know you exist?"

"I have no way of knowing."

Brandon looked exasperated. "Look, lovey, the man is gone. You'll get over it. Time is a great eraser. Before you know it, the only bloke you'll be thinking about is me!" He placed his hands on her shoulders. "See here, you beautiful, wonderful, stupid girl, I've changed my mind. I'm going to try being a father to this little bun you've got in the oven. Teach him power yoga and martial arts."

Catherine sensed a note of insincerity. *Is he kidding?* she thought.

Their eyes met, and he looked away. "This poor little nipper needs a dad, you know."

Catherine folded her arms and looked at him skeptically. "And what if 'he' is a 'she?'"

"Oh … well, girls are okay—"

There was an unexpected flash of yellow wings as a bird flew directly over Brandon's head. With a chirp and a flutter, a "bird bomb" landed on his shoulder. He stared down in horror at the spreading stain. "Oh, shit!" he exclaimed as Catherine stifled a giggle.

Brandon's father called from the porch of the ranch house. "Time to load up!"

"Better change the shirt," Catherine said and laughed.

A half hour later, the Skyhawk took off down the runway with Mr. McFarland at the controls. Peering out between pieces of luggage, Catherine watched as Brandon's mum frantically waved and grew smaller and smaller in the window. *What a lonely existence,* thought Catherine. *I don't think I could handle that.*

On the lawn in front of the ranch house, Bosco looked soulfully up at his mistress through mismatched eyes. Mrs. McFarland reached down to scratch him behind the ears, and the dog's tail thumped a drumbeat on the ground.

CHAPTER 39

The Letter

THINGS HAD GONE SMOOTHLY AT customs in Denpasar. Catherine Elizabeth Donovan's Indonesian visa had been extended for another six months. She knew she would have to apply for a new American passport within the year, for this one was running out. Still, she'd decided to worry about all that later. Who knows what the next twelve months would bring? For now, she was fine. She was safe in Bali, where she would await the arrival of her baby. The American embassy had assured her that the child was entitled to American citizenship.

Catherine had returned to her cottage at Namaste Yoga Retreat, not knowing exactly what to do about her relationship with Brandon. She was not in love with him, she knew that. Still, she didn't relish being a woman alone with a baby. He would protect them, of course, but what kind of a father would he be? On some instinctual level, she was convinced it would never work. Brandon really did not want this child, and that meant problems. If they had other children together, he might very well favor his own, and well … she just didn't want to go down that road.

Of course, life with Brandon would be decent, even adventurous at times. Solid relationships have been built on friendship alone. Still, time on this earth is so short. Was this the man she really wanted?

Catherine spent many wakeful nights debating these life-changing issues, and tonight was no exception. No matter how hard she tried, she simply could not sleep. She was becoming increasingly obsessed with memories of the night her baby had been conceived. She had not experienced anything like that ever in her life. How strange that it would occur in the midst of such a terrible tragedy.

Now that these erotic memories were surfacing, they put new barriers between her and Brandon.

The Australian was right, of course, when he said, "Is that man thinking of you? Does he even know you exist?" It was an issue she needed to address, but how could she do it? What would she say, and to whom?

So in the early morning hours, she arose from her sleepless bed and went to the small carved desk. The generator had been turned off for the night, so she lit a tall white candle that filled the space with the fragrance of jasmine. The candle sent a soft yellow light flickering around the high-ceilinged room. When she pulled open the desk drawer, she came upon an old-fashioned fountain pen and a blank piece of paper, and she placed them both on the surface in front of her. The paper was ivory in color and subtly embossed at the top with a single word, *Namaste*. The texture of the lettering felt like Braille beneath her fingers.

Catherine stared down at the paper, unsure of how to begin. As moonlight streamed in through the open window, the silence of the night was broken by the beautiful song of a bird.

Catherine looked up in surprise. *That must be a nightingale,* she thought. But it was a yellow canary sitting on a branch hidden beneath the leaves of the banyan tree. It ruffled its feathers and hopped about, warbling an aria with every fiber of its being.

On the limb beside him sat Katie, solemnly watching her mother through the cottage window.

Minutes passed with Catherine utterly lost in thought. Finally, she picked up the pen and began to write, and the silver point made small scratching sounds against the paper.

The message did not come quickly. Indeed, it was a slow process. Every sentence seemed of the utmost importance and had to be carefully weighed. By the time Catherine finished the letter, the hands on her small travel clock read four in the morning.

She signed her name as Catherine Scanlon, folded the paper into three equal parts, and slipped it into a blank envelope. After she carefully sealed the envelope, she wrote the name Nicholas on the front. Then she retrieved a newspaper clipping from the desk drawer and placed it together with the envelope.

After she blew out the candle, Catherine went back to bed. For the first time since she had returned from Australia, she fell quickly into a deep, dreamless sleep.

It was almost noon when Catherine awoke.

She sat bolt upright and thought, *Good heavens! I'll miss the jitney.* She tossed a beach dress over her head and ran up the path toward the road. In the distance, she could see the American student, Jennifer, standing next to the vehicle as the driver laboriously loaded suitcases into the back.

Catherine waved both arms and shouted, "Jennifer, wait!"

The girl turned and shaded her eyes against the brilliant midday sun. "Hold on. It's 'Lizbeth," she said to the driver. "This will just take a minute."

When Catherine ran up, Jennifer gave her a hug. "Glad you made it, 'Lizbeth. I hated to leave without saying good-bye."

"I have an unusual favor to ask," said Catherine. "Could you take this letter back to the States? I've got it right here." She handed over the letter and the scrap of newspaper.

"Of course," said Jennifer, smiling. Then she looked at the envelope. "But where do I send it? There's only one name on the front—"

"I'm asking you to find this man's last name and address. The details of the accident are all in the clipping. Just call the police station in Sarasota and get the name of the witness. His first name was Nicholas. I've written that on the front. The police must have the rest of his information on file somewhere." Catherine reached out to touch Jennifer on the arm. "This is very, very important. Will you do it?"

The girl grinned. "Of course I will! I love a woman of mystery!"

"And please, no return address on the letter."

"Understood." Jennifer placed her hand dramatically over her heart. "My lips are sealed. The mysterious Nicholas will never know from whence this letter came." Her voice dropped to a conspiratorial whisper. "And I promise I'll never, *ever* tell Brandon."

Catherine felt her face turn red. "Okay," she murmured.

Jennifer climbed into the jitney, and then she was off. Catherine watched the vehicle disappear from sight. As she walked slowly back toward her cottage, her thoughts were filled with one burning question: *Oh, Lord ... have I done the right thing?*

CHAPTER 40

The Unraveling

THREE WEEKS LATER ON A Saturday morning, the postman dropped the letter though a residential mail slot. It landed with a *thunk* on the living room floor of Nick's house in Sarasota.

Nick came shambling out of the kitchen in his pajamas, coffee mug in hand. He picked up the letter and studied the envelope. The name *Nicholas* was scripted in dark blue ink, while the last name and address were written in black ink and block letters. The smudged postmark read Cambridge, Massachusetts.

He frowned. "Cambridge? Who do I know in Cambridge?"

Nick walked back into the kitchen and set down his mug. He rummaged through a drawer for a knife and carefully slit open the envelope. As he unfolded the letter, he found a message handwritten on ivory paper in dark blue ink.

Dear Nicholas,

You were so kind to me after the tragic accident where I lost my beloved daughter, Katie. You gave me the gift of compassion and hope. I am writing because there is something I feel you ought to know. If I don't tell you now, I'm afraid I will never again find the strength to reveal it.

It is with joy that I tell you I am expecting your child.

I don't need anything. I don't want anything. I only hope that you'll think of me kindly and wish us both well. I live quite far away now, so I have asked a friend to find your address and mail this. Perhaps one day, I'll write you again. For now, this is enough.

I trust that you'll find it in your heart to welcome this news.

Catherine Scanlon

Stunned, Nick stared at the stationary on which the letter was written. The top of the paper was subtly embossed with a single word, *Namaste*. Nick touched the raised surface and felt the hair rise on the nape of his neck. A wave of anger swept over him. He strode to the phone, found the international number he had scribbled on a memo pad, and placed the call. It was early in the evening in Bali, and Brandon answered.

Nick launched his attack. "Okay, McFarland. I know beyond any shadow of a doubt that Catherine Scanlon is staying at your retreat. I want to talk to her right now. *Immediately!*" His fury was contagious, even halfway around the world.

Brandon's response was sarcastic. "Don't tell me. Let me guess. This has got to be Dr. Kontos."

"It is—"

"Well, guess what, ole buddy? There's no one here by the name of Catherine Scanlon."

Nick roared, "You're lying, McFarland. I *know* she's there!"

Brandon shouted back, "Get this straight, you crazy bastard. I'm telling you the truth! There's no Catherine Scanlon here. There's never been a Catherine Scanlon here, and no Catherine Scanlon is expected. How many times do I have to tell you that? Buzz off!" He slammed down the phone. "Jesus!"

In Candi Dasa, Brandon began pacing around his office in Candi Dasa. He was infuriated! Still, in spite what he'd said on the phone, questions began to ricochet inside his mind: Who was this damned Dr. Kontos? Was he some kind of stalker? Why did he keep calling? Who was this woman named Catherine Scanlon? Why was Kontos so sure she was here? And why was that idiot so desperate to find her?

Brandon stopped, took three deep breaths to calm himself, and then resumed pacing. *It makes no sense,* he muttered. *It makes no bloody sense at all!*

One by one, he recounted the facts. Not been many Americans had visited Namaste this year. The only American woman currently enrolled was Elizabeth Donovan. No one in their right mind would accuse 'Lizbeth of having long hair. It was barely three inches at most.

Still, hair can be cut … and names can even be changed.

Brandon froze in his tracks. *Oh, my God … what if this crazy Dr. Kontos is the sperm donor?*

Brandon marched over to 'Lizbeth's cottage, desperate to talk this out with her. When he got there, however, she was nowhere in sight. He pounded on the carved wooden door and called out her name, but the cottage remained silent.

With a mix of increasing wariness and dismay, Brandon pushed the door open and entered. He knew he shouldn't be doing that, but he had to get the situation resolved. Elizabeth Donovan was the name on her passport, he was certain of that. He'd seen that document at immigration. Why would she go by any other name unless, of course, she was running away from something? That Kontos guy had all the earmarks of a stalker. Maybe she had reason to be afraid.

As he scouted the cottage for clues, Brandon came upon the treasured snapshot of Katie. It sat on the bedside table, beautifully framed. It reminded him of the photos displayed on his mother's dresser. His Mum always put names and dates on the backs of photographs. Might 'Lizbeth have done the same?

Twisting the fasteners on the back, Brandon slipped the picture out of its frame. With a feeling of dread, he slowly turned it over.

Five words were inscribed on the back. As he read them, Brandon's hands began to shake.

Katie Scanlon, Lancaster, Age six.

His heart came to a screeching halt. "I'll be damned," was all he could think to say.

CHAPTER 41

The Scorn of a Rejected Woman

Afew days later, Lexi came to Nick's office at Gulf Marine Lab and waited for him to show up. Decked out in jeans and an Oscar de la Renta shirt, she impatiently paced the room, her Jimmy Choo steel stilettos leaving little dents in the wooden floor. As usual, she had arrived early that morning, while Nick was arriving late, of course. Lexi found her irritation growing by leaps and bounds. How could Nick be so stupid? At her urging, Daddy had given a major donation to support Nick's newest project. How *dare* he continue to blow her off!

Using his lateness as justification, Lexi began to poke around. She found nothing of interest on top of Nick's desk and nothing special in the center drawer or any of the other drawers for that matter. She decided to check out a wooden cupboard to the right of the desk. When she pulled the door open, Lexi discovered an array of photographs taped inside. They weren't the usual garage/mechanic/

calendar/bimbo shots. Instead, they were photos of a plainly dressed woman and what was obviously her child.

Thoughts raced through Lexi's head. *It's the girl with the Ubangi earrings. Attractive enough, I suppose, in an odd sort of way, but too bohemian for a class act like Nick. She's dressed like a Communist factory worker. Surely, he wouldn't fall for a woman like that!*

Lexi turned her critical eye to the pictures of the child. *Well, the girl's a pretty one, all right. Smiling, a little yellow bird perched on her shoulder. Looks a bit like her mother, except better dressed.*

When she returned to the photograph of the mother, Lexi missed a flash of yellow feathers.

She peered at the woman's face. *The bitch has great hair,* she thought begrudgingly. *Could use a few streaks and maybe something to take out the frizz.*

Turning her attention back to the child, Lexi was astonished to see that the kid was now scowling. She blinked her eyes and looked again. Sure enough, the girl was glaring straight into the camera.

Huh! Could have sworn the kid had a smile on her face—

She made a mental note to visit her optometrist and then turned her attention to the photo of two men, a snapshot of Nick and Marty, his assistant, on a recent dive trip in Greece. Both man brandished spear guns and were grinning broadly, their lean bodies bronzed and glistening. Nick had his free arm around Marty's shoulder, while Marty held up a hefty grouper. The snapshot was taped securely to the door, and Lexi ripped it off to examine it more closely. Squinting, she studied the shot as if it was a scientific specimen. Those guys were both great-looking men, but there was something off about the picture. Was it her imagination, or was Marty actually leaning up against Nick?

It all looked just a little too friendly.

Lexi thought of the demise of Dolores and Arnold. Her eyes narrowed, and her frown grew deeper.

Her speculation was interrupted by the crunch of tires rolling on gravel. Lexi pressed the snapshot back in place, closed the cupboard door, and trotted over to the window. From her vantage point, she could see Nick getting out of his Jeep and Marty running toward him from the dock. Their voices drifted through the glass.

Marty was first to speak. "Hey, boss! I just heard you were leaving."

"I am."

"How long you gonna be gone?"

"I have absolutely no idea."

"So you're off on another wild adventure! Well, I hope everything works out."

"So do I, buddy. So do I!"

The two men shook hands and embraced each other warmly. Lexi stared down from the office window. Dolores's words flashed through her mind: *That's the way it all began with Arnold. Just a simple bit of male bonding gone awry.*

A minute later, Nick entered the office, carrying his briefcase. He gave her the most impersonal of greetings. "Hi, Lexi, I'm late."

"Never knew you to be on time," was her vinegary reply.

Nick shrugged. "Hey, I'm Greek. We're historically late. Remember Odysseus?" Nick began sorting through documents on his desk, stuffing a few in his briefcase.

Lexi glared. "You're also historically bisexual."

He looked at her strangely and then laughed. "Ah! You noticed my pink underwear."

Smiling coldly, she watched as Nick went back to digging through his papers, putting most of them in the big file drawer of his desk. He opened the door to the wooden cupboard and began pulling off photos that were displayed inside, carefully removing the tape from the back of each, including the snapshot of Marty in Greece.

"Wouldn't want to forget that one," muttered Lexi, her voice dripping with acid.

Nick put the photos in his briefcase. "My, my, aren't we full of nasty little comments. You got some kind of problem?"

Lexi folded her arms and glared at him. "Indeed I do! This might seem like a *queer* question, Nick, but exactly what do you think you're doing?"

"I'm leaving for the island of Bali. Don't know how long I'll be gone." The briefcase closed with a loud snap.

She could feel her anger rising. "You're doing what?" Her hands jammed down on her hips. "What kind of gratitude is that? Have you forgotten? We're close to a deadline on a grant! Daddy has done everything possible to help get this project off the ground. There is *serious* money involved here, and you're taking off for some erotic fling in Indonesia?"

Nick stared at her. "Erotic? Hardly. Look, Lexi, I'm all burned out. No brain cells left." He pulled out a stack of manila file folders and thrust them toward her.

Lexi's voice was pure ice. "Dr. Kontos, this is *not* the time for you to take off on some stupid excursion!" She shoved the folders back across the desk.

Nick pushed the files back to her. "That's what *you* think, Dr. Knight. Too bad. I'm going. If we lose this grant, so be it. Your dad will simply have to understand. There will always be another grant around the corner."

Lexi was incredulous. "My dad? Understand? Are you kidding?"

Nick frowned. "We don't need his money, you know. It's nice to have, but we'll survive without it."

"How dare you say that about Papa? He's done so much!" The two glared at each other as they heaved the folders back and forth. Finally, Lexi shoved the pile with all her might, and manila folders spilled out all over the floor. "Well, so much for world hunger!" she snarled. Then she wheeled and stomped dramatically toward the door.

Nick sighed and ran his fingers through his hair. Reluctantly, he went after her, his tone conciliatory. "Oh, for God's sake, Lexi, you don't need me to finalize this grant. You're good! Finish it up. Marty will help."

She turned and glared haughtily at him. "Listen, lover boy, you've forgotten just how good I am!"

"Oh, come on. I'm talking about your research skills. Maybe you don't do everything yourself, but you certainly know how to make things happen. Hire help if you must. You've been doing that your entire academic life."

Lexi's eyes narrowed. "Listen, if you walk out on this project, I'll see that your reputation is dragged through the swamp and the gators eat you for breakfast. Your name will be toast!"

"Are you threatening me?"

"Yes, Nick, I am!" She turned to leave and then swiveled back. "Look, sex is the world's biggest motivator. There's got to be an outside person involved in this sudden exodus. So, tell me—what kind of twisted romantic involvement is compelling you to abandon our project and damage your career?"

Nick frowned. "I'm not abandoning this project. I'm putting it in your very capable hands. I've got plenty of unused vacation days. If I need to, I'll take a leave of absence. It's a personal thing, and believe me … it's important. I'm going to Bali, and, yes, there's someone I hope to find when I get over there."

"And exactly *who* might that person be?"

"None of your damned business!"

Lexi scowled like a prosecuting attorney. "It's clear you're ashamed."

Nick rolled his eyes. "Oh, God! I can't believe this conversation."

For Lexi, it was an aha moment. Convinced she had cracked Nick's code, she spoke in a voice that was laced with venom. "Is he *terribly* good-looking?"

Nick blinked. "I beg your pardon?"

"Why don't you and your Balinese boy toy send Daddy a postcard? He'll cross you right off his Christmas list." With that, Lexi gave Nick the finger and strode out the door in the style of a pissed-off Joan Crawford.

Nick was stunned. "What the hell was *that* all about?"

CHAPTER 42

The Ancient Art of Handwriting Analysis

CARRYING HIS NAVY BLUE DUFFLE bag, Nick emerged from the Denpasar Airport in Bali and looked around at the crowded street. The dusty road was jammed with motorbikes, cars, taxis, and pedestrians, and the sidewalks were filled with vendors hawking their wares. Like most crowded Asian marketplaces, everyone carried identical products: fabrics, shirts, blouses, shawls, sandals, carvings, hats, shell jewelry, spices, mementos, fruits, bottled water, and the like. If a tourist made the mistake of buying any one item, dozens of other peddlers would surge forward to press the exact same article on him again ... and again ... and again. It was colorful. It was energetic. It was a feeding frenzy of competitive hawkers hitting upon a handful of tourists and badgering them to the ground.

Nick had seen this all before in other parts of the world. He was here to find Catherine and nothing else. He quickly hailed a taxi and gave his destination. He settled the price in rupiahs and drove off toward the south, the beautiful waters of the Indian Ocean sparkling on his right. The crowded chaos of Denpasar faded in the rearview mirror as the friendly driver pointed out sights in broken English.

It was a beautiful island, all right, and Nick felt fortunate to be rested enough to appreciate it. As far as his flights from America had gone, they had been a slow-motion disaster. Shit happens, as they say in the business, and the damned trip had taken three days.

Stuck overnight in Jakarta, he was lucky to find a hotel and catch some shut-eye. By the time he boarded the plane to Denpasar, Nick felt reasonably rested and anxious to get on with his trip.

Now he was here, watching Balinese temples, villages, and water buffalo fly past the open window of the taxi. He admired the terraced rice fields and tall volcanoes and wondered what turn his life was about to take.

Nick could not be certain that he would find Catherine in Bali. The word *Namaste* was a common form of greeting that had been around for thousands of years. The only thing going for him was that Catherine had torn out a magazine ad for a place called Namaste in Candi Dasa. The evidence of her presence here was flimsy at best, but that was all he had to go on.

Nick stared out the window at passing villages. People walked by the side of the road dressed in the brilliant colors of Southeast Asia. Women wore fuchsia, bright yellow, poison green, hot pink, and electric purple, and they carried baskets of fruits and flowers on their heads. Children clutched simple toys, and men raced by on overloaded motorbikes, all against a backdrop of rice fields and coconut palms. It was a page right out of *Conde Nast Traveler*.

After he pulled Catherine's letter out from his bag, Nick read it for the ten-thousandth time. Receiving that letter had meant everything to Nick. From the moment he first sighted her at the Siesta Key Café, he knew she was unforgettable. Catherine and her beautiful daughter Katie had both struck a deep chord in his heart. There was even something about her handwriting that he found strangely compelling. She wrote in a large, handsome script, the kind you don't see in this age of computers. It reminded him of the type of handwriting his grandmother had had. To this day, he recalled his grandmother's bold script and the inspirational messages she inscribed on the birthday cards of his childhood.

To see writing like that was like hearing a voice. As Nick looked at the letter, he felt like Catherine was speaking the words: *I trust that you will find it in your heart to welcome this news.*

Oh, I welcome it, all right, thought Nick. *I welcome it more than you could ever imagine.*

The tropical scene outside the car window became blurred as Nick lapsed into memories of the remarkable night he had shared with Catherine so many months ago. Soon, he was lost in reverie and longing. He knew only one thing—that he had to find her. They had to bring this child into the world together. Then he'd go back to Gulf Marine and work out the other parts of his life, hopefully with Catherine. Maybe.

The taxi swerved to avoid a pothole, and Nick was abruptly jolted into reality. *Oh, knock it off, Kontos! What the hell are you doing? You're becoming a damned romantic freak.*

After he quickly refolded the letter, he shoved it back into his bag. Embarrassed, he looked at the taxi driver, but the Balinese man remained cheerfully oblivious.

CHAPTER 43

Beware the Devious Yogi

NICK STOOD IN THE DRIVEWAY of the Namaste Yoga Retreat, duffle in hand, his taxi vanishing down the road. Sighting this unexpected visitor, Brandon stepped out of the office and onto the porch. He looked at the stranger and frowned. "G'day, mate. What can I do for you?"

Nick set the duffle bag down on the step. "I'm looking for Catherine Scanlon."

Brandon did not even bother to smile. "Ah, Dr. Kontos, I presume. You're quite the persistent fellow. Well, as I've told you repeatedly, there's no one here by that name."

"I brought along a picture so you can see what she looks like." Nick pulled out the photo that had been pinned to his wall. It was the close-up of Catherine wearing earrings of filigreed gold, hair cascading over her shoulders. Brandon came down the steps to retrieve it. His nostrils flared as he examined the picture.

Brandon took a deep breath and willed his voice to hold steady.

Then he looked Nick dead in the eye and announced, "I would never forget a woman like that. The lady's a stranger."

Brandon abruptly handed back the photo and moved up the stairs. He was about to reenter the office when he turned. "Let me be clear, Dr. Kontos. I do not know that name. I do not know that face. I have never heard of this woman. You've come a long, long way to hear me repeat those statements."

Nick frowned. "You're right, McFarland. I *have* come a long way. Let's just say that finding this woman is extremely important to me."

Brandon's voice dripped with sarcasm. "Oh, I see! You've embarked upon the hero's journey."

Nick's eyes narrowed. "Call it what you want. I'm here."

Brandon folded his arms and tilted his head. "And would you say this trip falls under the category of unrequited love?"

"None of your damned business!" snapped Nick.

Brandon's eyes flickered. *Screw him,* he thought. *I'm going to get rid of this guy!* Determined to appear detached, Brandon moved toward the office door, motioning Nick to follow. "Please. Come in."

Nick climbed the stairs and entered. Once inside, Brandon indicated a wall chart showing names and cottage numbers. "Check out our roster. There's no one here by the name of Catherine. There's no one here by the name of Scanlon. Look for yourself. I'll be back in a minute."

As Nick studied the chart, Brandon ran down the steps and into the adjacent cottage, which served as the kitchen. There, he found the houseboy, Wayan Pedjeng, who was eating a bowl of curried rice. Brandon spoke in a low voice. "Wayan, there's a man here from America. A very bad man. He's crazy. He wants to kidnap 'Lizbeth."

A look of horror came across Wayan's face. "Kidnap?"

"The stupid bloke has a picture of 'Lizbeth. It was taken a long, long time ago. Go talk to him. If he shows you the picture, you must say you do not know her. He may call her by some other name, but he is very, very dangerous. He wants to take her back to America."

Wayan stood to his full five feet and scowled, "I no let him kidnap 'Lizbeth. I stab him with my kris!"

Brandon shook his head. "No stabbing. No swords."

Wayan declared resolutely, "I no let bad man kidnap 'Lizbeth!"

Brandon put his hand on the boy's shoulder. "Right. But let words be your weapons. Go talk to him. Get him off her track."

Wayan nodded.

After he scampered over to the office, Wayan found Nick scrutinizing the list of names and cottage numbers. The boy took the stance of a demon dancer, legs wide apart and arms folded.

Nick looked at the slight young man. "Do you work here?" he asked.

"I am head houseboy," Wayan declared with great pride.

"I see. Well, do you know of a lady named Catherine?"

Wayan solemnly shook his head.

Nick pressed on. "Maybe she's called Mrs. Scanlon?"

The houseboy shook his head more sternly.

Nick expanded his description. "Mrs. Catherine Scanlon, American, long hair, about this tall—" He held his hand at her approximate height.

Wayan scowled fiercely and shook his head even harder.

Nick held out the snapshot. "Perhaps you recognize this picture?"

The boy gave it a cursory glance and pushed it dramatically aside. "No. No, Cat'rin here. I never meet Cat'rin. Nobody here ever look like that."

"You're certain?"

The houseboy nodded emphatically. "Yes. Sure. No Cat'rin."

Nick sighed. "I thought, of course, she'd be here," he murmured.

Wayan widened his eyes and glared. "Long-hair-picture lady not here! Never here! No!"

As Nick stared at the ferocious young man, his confidence began to wither. Maybe Catherine's letter had been written somewhere else. Maybe the *Namaste* thing was pure coincidence. Maybe she wasn't here in Bali after all.

With Wayan assigned to the role of guard dog, Brandon hurried down the path in search of Merpati. He found her at last in a nearby hut and spoke to her in a conspirator's urgent voice. "Go find 'Lizbeth. Take her up to the temple ruins. Tell her to stay put 'til I get there. Something crazy's going on. I'll explain later."

Merpati's eyes grew large as saucers. She gave a small nod and ran off toward the village.

As fate would have it, Catherine had not gone toward town. Instead, she had headed for Iwayan's cottage, where she and Lastri were now entertaining the baby out on the porch. As Catherine lifted the little boy onto her lap, the gold around his neck and wrists and ankles glittered in the sun. Smiling, Catherine bounced him gently on her knee and began to chant little nursery rhymes. As she did so, her thoughts were of Katie and the games they had played and the songs they had sung.

> *Humpty Dumpty sat on a wall.*
> *Humpty Dumpty had a great fall.*
> *All the king's horses and all the king's men*
> *couldn't put Humpty together again."*

Iwayan laughed with glee as Catherine jiggled him up and down.

Suddenly, the boy stiffened his legs and froze. He stared at girl in a tall golden hat who had appeared near the top of the banyan tree.

Puzzled, Catherine studied Iwayan's astonished face. "What are you looking at, honey?"

Tilting his head and sucking his thumb, the wordless child could only gape, mesmerized by the antics of a tiny yellow bird.

Swiveling to follow the little boy's gaze, Catherine caught a blur of yellow feathers out of the corner of her eye. Iwayan saw it too, and a tidal wave of laughter engulfed him. He grabbed at Catherine's dangling earring and tugged on it with all his might. "Ouch!" she cried. She slipped it off and rubbed her ear. "You're strong for a little guy," she whispered.

Giggling, Iwayan stretched out his fingers once again to reach for her last remaining earring. Catherine reared back, laughing. "No, no, sweetheart. You've got plenty of jewelry all your own!" When he turned to his mother, she said, "You'd better hold these for me, Lastri."

As Lastri held out her hand, a voice was heard calling, "Miss 'Lizbeth— Miss 'Lizbeth—" The women looked up to see Merpati running breathlessly toward them.

At the cottage that also served as the office, Wayan remained fiercely on guard. Nick kept busy studying names on the wall chart until Brandon finally returned.

"Find anything?" asked Brandon.

Nick shook his head. "You're right, of course. Her name's not there. Nonetheless, I still have the feeling she's somewhere nearby."

Brandon frowned. "Interesting. Why do you think that?"

"Fate. Destiny. Synchronicity. Why don't *you* tell *me*? You're the man who's into all that mystical mind stuff."

Brandon shrugged. "Not really. I'm in the business of buffing up bodies. Power yoga's my specialty. It's a fitness thing. My students want a serious workout with minimum chanting and meditation." Brandon stopped to stare pointedly at his watch. "Matter of fact, I've got a class in twelve minutes. So … is there anything else I can do for you?"

Nick frowned. *Why* did he not trust this guy? "Show me the grounds."

"Why should I? I've got classes. I don't have time to give you a tour."

"Well then, what's the chance of my staying here for a few days?"

Brandon folded his arms. "Not possible. We're completely booked."

Nick motioned toward wall chart. "Really? You've got two slots on that chart with no names."

Brandon glared. "Those cottages are under construction."

"I see. Well … is there another place nearby where I could stay?"

"There's an old inn half an hour down the road. The Bulan Purnama. Can't recommend it. Pretty shoddy." Brandon looked again at his watch. "And now, Dr. Kontos, it's time for me to meet my class. I have no place for you to stay. There is no Catherine Scanlon. Perhaps the person you're searching for is pure illusion."

Nick had to admit the man had a point. It was reckless to have traveled so far with so little evidence. Still, Brandon came off like a jerk. The hostility between the two men was palpable. Brandon strode off toward the yoga platform without so much as a handshake.

No love lost here, thought Nick. After he picked up his duffle, he walked out to the congested road and flagged down a taxi. "Do you speak English?"

"Yes, sir," said the driver proudly. "Where you want to go?"

Nick shrugged. "Do you know anything about an old inn down the road?"

"The Bulan Purnama? It closed. Will tear down and build new."

Huh, thought Nick. *One more reason not to trust McFarland.* When he turned back to the driver, he asked, "Know of any other place I could stay?"

The man shrugged. "Small place in rice paddies. Six, maybe eight kilometers away. But best place is Ubud. Americans like Ubud. Very pretty. Get there in one hour."

Nick shook his head. "Too far. Let's head for the place in the rice paddies." He got in, and the taxi pulled out into clogged traffic.

They had moved perhaps fifty feet down the road when there was a sharp, cracking sound. A ramshackle lorry had broken its axle. With a metallic screech, the enormous vehicle teetered slowly over onto one side, completely blocking the road and filling it with dust. People came running from every direction as the driver crawled out, apparently unharmed. Cars and motorbikes began jockeying to get past the overturned lorry, but few could get much of anywhere. Nick's taxi was stalled, locked in by a thicket of vehicles.

Nick stared at the crowd and wondered what he could do to help.

Not far behind the taxi, a woman strode down the sidewalk, a child in a sling on her back.

Nick's attention was riveted on the snarl of traffic that jammed the road ahead. He asked the driver, "Wonder if we could gather enough men to push the lorry to one side?"

The man shook his head. "Big truck. Very heavy."

Nick looked out at the sea of brown faces. *The Balinese are a handsome people,* he thought. Then to his amazement, he caught sight of the pale skin of a young Western child. It was a girl who was maybe six or seven years of age, wearing flowered jeans and a sky blue shirt. Nick gasped. *My God! That kid looks just like Katie.* The child turned, looked him straight in the eyes, and smiled. Astonished, Nick opened the car door and jumped out into the crowded street, but the girl had vanished.

Dumbstruck, Nick sank back down into the taxi, immune to the sounds of honking horns. *Oh, great! Now I'm losing it,* he thought.

The woman had now caught up with the taxi. She passed within inches of Nick's window, golden earrings flashing like fishing lures.

Nick mulled over the apparition of Katie that he had just seen.

The woman stepped in front of the Nick's taxi and paused. There was a flurry of yellow wings and a soft thud as a small bird crashed into the windshield. *"Hei Beruang! Hati-hati!"* yelled the driver.

The disoriented animal fell back awkwardly onto the hood of the car and hopped around on one claw, chirping. Nick stared at the yellow bird. *What the blazes is a canary doing out here?*

Nick watched in disbelief as the bird danced across the hood of the car. Suddenly, a glint of gold caught his attention. His eyes refocused to include the woman and the jewelry she was wearing. Abruptly, Nick leapt out to the sidewalk and grabbed the woman's arm. "Where did you get those earrings?"

Alarmed, she pulled back, and the baby began to cry.

His voice was gruff. "Those earrings—where did you get them?"

The woman's hand flew to her cheek. "Lizbeth. She leave them in my house at Namaste. I no steal earrings." The woman moved defensively away as the baby wailed louder and louder. "I give back when I see her."

Nick's voice softened. "Of course you will, of course. But you say they belong to Elizabeth, not Catherine?"

"'Lizbeth. I never meet no Cat'rin."

"Elizabeth—"

The baby continued to blubber.

Nick suddenly came to his senses. "I am so sorry," he said to the woman. "I didn't mean to frighten you or your child. Please forgive me."

When he turned back toward the taxi, Nick shoved a few thousand rupiah through the window at the driver. He grabbed his duffle bag from the backseat and announced, "I'm going back. Keep the change."

CHAPTER 44

When the Heart Is Ready, the Lover Will Come

NICK RAN ALONG THE CROWDED sidewalk toward the entrance to the Namaste Yoga Retreat. He went through the gate, turned down the path, tossed his duffle bag on the office steps, and strode angrily toward the platform where Brandon was about to start his class in power yoga. Today's group was made up of a dozen international students, all having arrived in Bali that very morning. It was Brandon's first chance to meet them.

The Aussie looked up to see Nick rapidly approaching and groaned, "Start doing warm-ups. I've got some unfinished business." As the students dutifully unraveled their yoga mats, their eyes remained glued on their departing instructor.

The two men caught up to each other some twenty feet down the path. Nick was first to speak, and he was furious. "Okay, McFarland, I want the truth. Exactly who is the woman named Elizabeth?"

Brandon ran a hand through his thicket of hair. "Ah, well, I think I just got my lesson in fate, destiny, and synchronicity."

Incensed, Nick stood, hands on hips. "Go on. Continue—"

"'Lizbeth Donovan is a beautiful American. She's been here about five months. She's the woman I hope to marry. And—" Brandon took a deep breath and continued, "She happens to be pregnant."

"Yours?"

Brandon shook his head. "No, the kid's not mine, but that's no matter. I'd take care of him just the same and of 'Lizbeth."

Oh, Christ, thought Nick in a sudden flash of insight. *The guy's in love with her. That's why he's been behaving like such a colossal jerk.*

Nick felt calmness come over him. "This 'Lizbeth—could her real name be Catherine? Catherine Scanlon?"

Brandon glared defiantly. "That's not the name she's been using!" He began to pace back and forth, clenching and unclenching his fists.

From their vantage point on the platform, the eyes and ears of the yoga students remained riveted on the confrontation.

Abruptly, Brandon halted and glared at Nick. "Damn it! Why did you have to show up?"

"Exactly what do you mean by that?"

"Why didn't you just stay put? 'Lizbeth and I've been getting on great. I'm okay with her having a kid. We're a team. We make a great couple." Inhaling deeply, Brandon's voice escalated into a shout. "You bloody Yank, you're screwing up my life!"

The eyes of the yoga class shifted toward Nick. "Really!" he yelled. "Well, you've sure done a great job of screwing up mine! You've been lying to me for weeks!"

Lying? The students looked at each other.

"You son of a bitch!" Enraged, Brandon took a flying swing at Nick, who ducked, barely escaping the blow. Brandon danced around like a boxer, hands raised, ready to strike. "I want you *out* of here!" he bellowed.

Nick stood his ground. "Cool it," he muttered.

"Cool it?" roared Brandon. "I'll cool *you*, you bloody ratbag!" He spun around twice and aimed a karate kick at his opponent. Nick saw it coming and dodged to one side. The kick tore his shirt as it grazed past his shoulder.

The students gasped, and several leapt to their feet.

Nick folded his arms. "Okay, I got it. You're a black belt."

"I am," said Brandon, his voice irate.

"Well, believe it or not, dickhead, I did *not* come here to get involved in some school-yard fight. I came to find the woman who is carrying my child."

The eyes of the students widened.

Brandon looked startled. He froze for a moment and then lowered his hands. "And what makes you think you're the father?"

"She wrote to me."

Brandon blinked, and his voice flooded with disbelief. "Did she tell you to come here?"

"No, but she sure didn't tell me to stay away!" Nick was exaggerating. He knew full well he had not been invited.

Brandon's eyes narrowed. "I can't believe that 'Lizbeth would write you."

"Well, she did."

The Aussie seemed incredulous. "She actually sent you a letter?"

Nick patted his shirt pocket. "Yep, I've got it right here," he said as he nodded, hoping the man would not ask to see it.

Brandon turned. His shoulders slumped, and he seemed to deflate. "Oh, shit!" he mumbled. Moments passed before he said anything else, and when he spoke, his voice was flat and dejected. "It seems like the lady wasn't *quite* as happy as I thought—"

"Sure looks that way," exclaimed Nick. Privately, he thought, *I ought to send this guy* A Dummies Guide to Women.

Brandon stared out toward the mountain, frozen in place, apparently lost in thought. Nick bided his time. One by one, the students sank down to their mats and resumed doing stretches. As they did, however, their eyes remained glued on the skirmish.

At last, Brandon turned to face the American. "You win, Dr. Kontos. Go talk it out with 'Lizbeth. You're pretty much a stranger in her life. Go find out what she really has to think."

Relief washed over Nick. He felt like he'd just defeated a dragon. "Fair enough," he said, and he nodded. "So where do I find her?"

"Follow me." Brandon led Nick to a bend in the path where the vista opened to gardens and farmlands with the outline of a volcano etched on the distant horizon. Brandon pointed toward the remnants of a small temple perched at the top of terraced rice fields. "I think you'll find your Catherine Scanlon up there." With obvious reluctance, the Aussie thrust out his hand. "If it turns out she thinks you're the bloke of her dreams, well … take care of her, mate."

"I promise," said Nick.

The two men looked at each other and begrudgingly shook hands.

Brandon wheeled abruptly and returned to his class. As he climbed the steps to the platform, he could feel twelve pairs of students' eyes riveted upon him. When he reclaimed his mat at the front, he announced: "Ladies and gentlemen, fasten your seat belts. You are about to embark upon the power yoga trip of your life."

Off he went through a series of fast-moving asanas, yoga poses that were worthy of the Olympics. With stern concentration, Brandon focused his attention on performing powerful, fluid moves. As he did so, he deliberately pushed away all thoughts of 'Lizbeth and the hopes he had held for their life together. As his fierce, athletic poses went deeper and deeper, his dreams of 'Lizbeth began to fade. He'd known that they would, for he'd done this before, many more times than he cared to remember.

The class was intense and strenuous, and it went on for a full ninety minutes. It was all too much for three of the new inductees, who quietly slipped off the platform and headed off to collapse on the beach. By the end of the workout, the nine surviving students were both exhausted and exhilarated.

As the group began rolling up their yoga mats, a slim blonde Norwegian girl walked over to Brandon. She put her hand on his forearm and stared at him with glacier blue eyes.

"Mr. McFarland," she whispered, "at times like this, you must remember that when the heart is ready, the lover will come."

Startled, Brandon stepped back and stared at the girl. "Bloody right!" he exclaimed. "Now what did you say your name was?"

CHAPTER 45

Lovers in Paradise

WHILE BRANDON VIGOROUSLY DROWNED HIS sorrows in a thousand asanas, Nick began his solitary journey toward the temple ruins overlooking the yoga retreat. The ruins were perhaps a mile away, and he was glad to have time to himself to gather his thoughts. As he walked along a path at the base of the stair-stepped rice fields, his mind flooded with feelings.

He had spent only hours with this woman named Catherine, and yet their lives had become inextricably linked. Even if she had not written that letter, Nick knew he would have continued to hunt for her for the rest of his life. He would have never stopped searching, for in his heart of hearts, he felt they were destined to be together.

Nick would never forget the first time he'd seen her at the Siesta Key Café. At first glance, she was but another pretty waitress. Then she turned to look at him, and *bam!* He felt he was looking at Helen of Troy. Perhaps it had been her long swath of hair caught up in a clip. Or perhaps it had been the earrings, which might well have belonged to an ancient royal princess. Whatever it was, he'd known right away that Catherine was someone special.

At least he knew she was special to him.

There was the extraordinary night they had spent wrapped in each other's arms. How could such an evening of heartbreak turn into something so beautiful? It made no sense, but it had. And why would this ephemeral encounter bring a child into being? *In a few short moments, our worlds were changed.*

Nick felt it had been fated to happen.

And then there was little Katie. She'd been so bright and quick and playful, and she seemed to genuinely like him. Nick grinned as he recalled the announcement she had made to her mother: *"He'd make a very good daddy."* Although Nick couldn't see Catherine's face at the time, he knew without question she had to be blushing.

Katie was right, Nick said to himself. *I would make a good father. I never thought I'd feel that way, but it's certainly a part of why I'm here.*

He had traveled perhaps two hundred yards up the rocky path before his thoughts were interrupted by a series of quacks. A farmer rushed down the mountain in pursuit of his runaway flock. As Nick waited for the ducks to pass, he took a moment to look around. For the first time, he noticed that water buffalo were plowing the fields and children were flying brightly colored kites. Balinese women were tending their rice, their faded work clothes providing splashes of muted color. Verdant life bloomed all around him, and the air was filled with the scent of earth. *Gauguin might have painted this scene,* he thought. *It's as lush as the Garden of Eden.*

The path toward the ruins grew quite steep. He had not climbed much farther before a little girl came scrambling toward him, clutching a brilliant yellow kite. As they passed one another, she looked directly into his eyes. For one brief moment, her face looked exactly like Katie's.

Nick came to a halt. *They'd be about the same age,* he thought as he stared at the apparition. In his mind, he could hear Katie's very last words: "Will you take care of me?"

"Yes— Yes—" he had promised.

"And my mommy?"

"Of course. Whatever you want."

At the moment of her death, he had given his word, and now he was here to carry out that promise.

He turned toward the girl with the yellow kite. She glanced back at him over her shoulder and smiled. He watched transfixed as she tossed her kite into the air and tugged on the string. The dazzling yellow paper caught the wind. It lunged and plunged and was sucked toward the sky, where it joined other multicolored comets snapping across the emerald sea of rice.

A small yellow bird appeared out of nowhere and landed on the little girl's shoulder. Nick stared at the creature and caught his breath. *The snapshot of Katie— The golden canary—*

The ruins at the top of the hill now loomed overhead, and Catherine appeared at the temple entrance. After he had searched for her for so many months, Nick froze in his tracks, and his heart began pounding.

This was it. This was the moment for which he had waited.

The breeze ruffled her short dark hair and pressed against her loosely wrapped sarong of magenta and green. As she stood silhouetted against the windswept sky, Nick saw that her body was swelling with child. She looked first toward the undulating fields of rice and then slowly turned and saw him. She shaded her eyes as she watched him approach.

"Catherine! Catherine!" Nick shouted as he broke into a run.

Her hands flew to her face. "Nicholas?" She closed her eyes for one brief moment and then stepped forward, her arms extended. Nick leapt up the broken steps two at a time. He gathered her into his arms and swung her around and around, hearing joy in her laughter. When he set her back down, he took both of her hands into his and felt a bolt of electricity pass between them.

Catherine looked at Nick in amazement. "How did you ever find me?" she asked.

His gaze held steady. "I've never been able to forget you, Catherine. It's just that simple. I promised I would come to you."

"And here you are," she added softly.

Nick nodded. *She is so beautiful,* he thought, and he laughed in delight. "I've come to tell you that I feel like I've loved you forever. I'm ecstatic to know that we're having a child."

Tears started to spill down her cheeks, and Nick wiped them away with his finger.

Then he reached into his pocket and fished out the tiny gold Katie necklace. "I've kept this for a long time. If we're having a girl, she gets to wear it." He coiled the necklace slowly down into her palm and folded her fingers over it.

"Of course she will," Catherine whispered.

Everything about this moment feels right, thought Nick. They stared into each other's eyes and slowly fused into a passionate embrace.

The specter of Katie appeared at the temple door, Mr. Sunshine perched upon her finger. As she gazed at Catherine and Nick, the child broke into melodious laughter.

Katie raised her arm toward the sky, and Mr. Sunshine flew away, now free. He flitted and wheeled above her head. She blew him a kiss, and together, they faded into the bright light of the sun.

Twelve weeks later, Katie Kontos returned to the world—born to the parents she had so carefully chosen.